LEVON'S RANGE

A VIGILANTE JUSTICE THRILLER BOOK 11

CHUCK DIXON

ROUGH EDGES PRESS

ROUGH EDGES PRESS

Paperback Edition
Copyright © 2022 Chuck Dixon

All rights reserved. No part of this book may be reproduced by any means without the prior written consent of the publisher, other than brief quotes for reviews.

This book is a work of fiction. Any references to historical events, real people or real places are used fictitiously. Other names, characters, places and events are products of the author's imagination, and any resemblance to actual events, places or persons, living or dead, is entirely coincidental.

Published in the United States by Wolfpack Publishing, Las Vegas

Rough Edges Press
An Imprint of Wolfpack Publishing
5130 S. Fort Apache Rd. 215-380
Las Vegas, NV 89148
roughedgespress.com

Paperback ISBN 978-1-68549-123-9
eBook ISBN 978-1-68549-122-2
LCCN 2022939238

LEVON'S RANGE

LEVON'S RANGE

1

After twenty years or more as an Idaho land agent, Tina Needham was used to long drives. She'd even come to enjoy them.

What she did not like was long silences.

Her current client offered little in the way of conversation. Not a big chit-chatter. No fan of small talk. He just sat like a sphinx on the passenger side of her Tahoe with his eyes on the brow of mountains shimmering under a cloudless sky to the west.

"I heard a bit of a drawl," she said to fill the void. "My husband and I are from Richmond originally."

"We're out here from Pascagoula," Levon Cade lied.

"What brings you west?"

"My wife passed a while back. Cancer. I thought a change would do my girls good." That had the advantage of being half true.

"Big change. This property is pretty remote."

"We lived rural in Mississippi. They're used to it."

"Do your daughters like horses?"

"No, ma'am," Levon offered a hint of a smile.

"They love horses."

"You're renting that place I picked you up at?" A three bedroom on a quarter acre in a sub-division outside Carey.

"Yes, ma'am. It's a little cramped with me and the two girls and their grandfather."

"I can see why you're looking for more space."

Tina turned her truck to make a right onto a hardpack road of crushed stone. The entry to the road was marked by a battered mailbox on a concrete post. The truck raised rooster tails of dust behind it. The land rose here, the peaks of the mountains seeming to recede into the ground as the Tahoe climbed the slope.

"The property is along this road?" Levon asked.

"It started back at the county road," Tina said, fixing Ray-Bans to her nose. "Soon as I turned off. This would be your road if you buy."

They topped a hillock and could see miles of open prairie where it dropped away toward the base of the mountains in the far distance. The road ran down the backslope to cut through the grass to where the steel rooftops of some buildings reflected the afternoon sun with a white sheen.

"It's fifty-two acres," she said as she navigated the rutted roadway. "But it sits like a notch cut out of federal land. Open range. You're surrounded on three sides by over a hundred thousand acres of grazable government property. Twenty or so acres are fenced though it's been a while since I've been out here. I can't swear to the condition of the fencing. You have a neighbor five miles to the north and another eight miles south."

"A house and barn?" Levon asked, putting on his

own shades against the harsh light of the lowering sun.

"A four-bedroom rancher built in the '60's by the original owner. Steel barn that's maybe twenty years old. And some other outbuildings. Like the fencing, I can't speak to the condition."

Tina drove between posts over which an arched sign was mounted. "Elysium" was carved into the curved oak beam. The tires sang over cattle guards set in the road surface across the gate opening.

"Original owner was a scholar. Or a romantic," she said. "Or maybe his wife was."

The truck drew up into a broad yard between a low-roofed, single-story building and a two-story barn of green-painted steel. A trio of Sierra pines grew to one side of the house. The yard was dotted with clutches of spiny brambles. A beard of yellowing weeds grew up around the foundations of the house and barn. A New Holland tractor and a manure spreader sat in a tangle of tall weeds rusting away. An El Camino that looked to be held together by prayer and primer rested on blocks next to the barn. An open-front stable building was set against the back fence line. There was a well house and a windmill set above it.

"A creek runs across the back of the property but it's not reliable." Tina glanced at her cheat sheet as they climbed from the cab. "The well's been tested and runs sweet. But it's not going to be enough for cattle. That's why the price is so good. Lowest per-acre being asked in county."

"We're not looking to raise livestock," Levon said. "Just a few horses."

He stood scanning the horizon, looking past the

house and other structures to the empty land that lay beyond. Nothing to see but an expanse of waving grass all the way to where it faded to a haze at the lap of the Rockies.

"The house has a propane heater and a wood-fired furnace. You'll need to lay in about twenty cords or more for the cold months," Tina said as she stepped toward the house. "And the septic will need pumping, I imagine."

It wasn't until she stepped up onto the flags of the front veranda that she realized she was alone. She turned to see that Mr. Holman, as she knew him, was already at the barn and sliding the big hangar doors open.

"Horse people," she smiled to herself. "Every time."

2

Sheriff Elmo Struthers wondered why in hell he bothered to pick up an x-large coffee at the Circle K on his way into the office. The last thing he needed was a hot drink. It wasn't even nine o'clock in the morning and already the AC was losing its battle to the Bama humidity. His shirt was sticking wetly to his back.

"Dina," he called. "Can you bring me in a bottle of water from the break room?"

He heard voices in the outer office. Dina's shrill protests and a deeper, male, voice.

"I'm sorry, Sheriff," Dina called as Roland Taggart shouldered the door open.

"It's all right, Dina," Elmo stood up from his desk with a smile to greet his red-faced visitor. Though it damned sure *wasn't* all right.

"What you doin' about my boy?" Taggart shouted, ignoring the sheriff's invitation to take the guest chair.

"I sent out notices like I told you, Rolly."

"Two weeks ago!" Rolly punched the desktop

unsettling a messy pile of reports. "And you ain't done jack shit since then."

"That's not true and you know it," Elmo said, drawing the spilled pile together. "I sent my deputies around to Deacon's usual places. No one's seen him or heard from him. I tried tracing that cell phone you gave me and came up empty. I sent a report on to state CID."

"And Dougie Clawson! His wife's worried sick. Callin' night and day. Wherever Deke is, Dougie's with him."

Of that there was no doubt, Elmo thought to himself. Deacon Taggart and Doug Clawson were, most times, joined at the hip. One thinking of ways to get into trouble the other hadn't thought of yet. More than likely, the pair had done something particularly felonious and had lit out of the county till things cooled off. Rolly was probably only in here playacting the grieving daddy while his son and his asshole buddy were sleeping one off in a Birmingham cathouse.

"And what about his Traverse?" Rolly said, knuckles on the desktop.

Elmo blinked at that one.

"His truck! His Chevy! You lookin' for that?" Rolly whined.

"Yeah. I told you so," Elmo nodded. "We put a BOLO out on it. It hasn't shown up anywhere."

"BOLOs and notices and reports! That's all bullshit. Next you gonna put Deke's picture on a milk carton?"

Better on bottles of Jack given the junior Taggart's social circle, Elmo thought. Instead of voicing this he said:

"What is it you'd like me to do?"

"Have you even taken a ride out to the Cades? Their place down off Sawmill."

"And why would I do that?"

"'Cause me and the Cades had some trouble recently. That boy Levon jacked Deke up. There's bad blood going a ways back."

Generations, Elmo recalled. The Cades and Taggarts had been bitter enemies so long the origins of their rancor had been forgotten. Nobody held a grudge like these hillbillies. Not even the mafia. If Levon had tuned up the Taggart boy it was pure D deserved. Of that Elmo was certain.

"Well, if it'd make you settle down I'll take a run out and talk to them."

"Good luck with that, Sheriff. They've run off."

"What's that mean?"

"I mean what I mean. They're alla them gone. Their vehicles and dogs too. Even the horses are gone."

"How long back?"

"More'n a week."

Elmo considered this while Rolly ranted on, pacing the carpet.

"I'll look into it," Elmo said, standing and taking his jacket down from the rack.

"You want me to go with you?" Rolly said, backing to the door.

"It's better if you didn't," Elmo said, using his lawman voice, part professional authority, part sincere concern. But the pure truth was, he couldn't stand Roland Taggart or his pain-in-the-ass son and wanted out of his company.

"Radio me if anything comes up, Dina," he said

as he sailed past her desk and out to his unmarked unit thinking more of snagging an iced coffee at the WaWa than any real investigation.

***

Taggart had not exaggerated.

Elmo found the yard and garage at the Cade place empty of cars or trucks. The house lay open and unlocked. No one answered his calls or knocks. He pulled on a pair of blue vinyl gloves. Reminding himself to secure a warrant later, he stepped into the kitchen. Cabinets stood open with some shelves empty. The dog bowls were missing from a mat on the faded linoleum floor. Throughout the house there were signs of hasty packing. Closets stood open and bookshelves had empty spaces free of dust. The master bedroom had a section of flooring pulled up. In the family room a gun safe lay open, stripped to the walls except for an old cleaning kit and a few stray boxes of .410 ammo.

The barn was the same. Wide open and free of any animals, the stalls chained open. The garage had walls of tools hanging with a few pegs empty. The only secured building was a steel shed the approximate size of a doublewide. This was windowless with a heavy brass padlock on the reinforced door. He'd need a warrant for that. And deputies.

He was back the next morning with three deputies, the entire shift and one man held over from third watch. While they searched the wooded acres, Elmo cut the lock to the shed.

Inside was a workshop with re-loading equipment and a high-end metal lathe. There was another gun safe here, also open, and mostly empty. Of greatest interest was an empty desk area that, as far as Elmo could surmise, had been a computer workstation. There was no keyboard or mouse. The monitor and printer remained along with a CPU tower that was turned on the desktop with its casing off and its hard drives removed. He could find no indication of a cable and he knew for damned sure there was no internet available up this holler. There were no discs or files or papers of any kind either on the shelves above the desk or in the drawers of any of the file cabinets. There was a device unknown to him that sat trailing loops of cable. Upon studying it he determined it was used for converting VHS tapes to some kind of digital format. There were no videotapes anywhere in the shed and he could not recall finding any in the house.

He stepped wincing into the sunlight as Jack Breem, one of his men, trotted across the yard for him.

"Found something in the woods," Jack said. "A new Chevy."

3

The car was a Chevrolet Traverse and registered to Deacon Elias Taggart.

That was enough for Elmo Struthers to declare the Cade farm a crime scene and shoo his deputies out of the woods while he called in the staties.

Two CID men arrived that evening and did as much of an assessment as they could in the failing light. A sweep of the house and surrounds turned up blood evidence in the yard in a few places. They'd need analysis to determine of it was human or otherwise.

The forensics bus arrived from Montgomery the next morning. Within hours the house and the buildings and woods all around were marked out with yellow tape. Techs dressed like spacemen were tramping around poking and prodding and collecting samples. The Traverse was painted inside and out with fingerprint powder and photographed like a swimsuit model.

Things got more interesting when a K-9 team arrived with the cadaver sniffing dogs. A pair of bloodhounds set up a fuss over a patch of ground that lay among some beeches well up in the hills behind the property. An excavation team uncovered two relatively fresh bodies, adult males, lying together in a six foot grave and wrapped in heavy plastic covered over with quicklime. The hole was a neatly dug rectangle and as professional an interment as any of the team had seen in their careers of uncovering remains.

Prints determined that the men were indeed Deacon Taggart and his asshole buddy Douglas Dawson. Both had a sheaf of priors and their prints were on file with the county and state.

"So, we're looking at a double homicide and the folks we're looking for have a two-week head start," Elmo said to one of the CID detectives. Henderson? Hemingway?

"Well, it wasn't suicide," Henderson or Hemingway said. "Two weeks and they're out of the state. Far off our patch, anyway."

"Out of the country even," Elmo said and thought of the section of pulled up floorboards at the house. They'd also come across freshly dug holes all over the back acres and one in the paddock. Some had rusty coffee cans discarded nearby. Sure as shit they weren't full of buttons.

"In any case, it's interstate flight," Henderson or Hemingway said. "All we can do is gather what we have and present it to the feds."

"This used to be a quiet county. Long as I've been sheriff anyway. Only the last year or so it's been one thing followed by another."

"You know this family?"

"Only by reputation."

"What about the dead men? I see a lot of convictions in their background."

"A pair of jokers. Their daddies are both in the shine business. Them too most probably. Put them both together and the sum total equals one halfwit."

"So, we done here or just getting started?" the CID man said.

"Just leave everything where it is except for the deceased, leave your tape and markers and I'll make the phone calls," Elmo said. "Unless you want to."

"Your county, Sheriff," Henderson or Hemingway said with a crooked smile.

By late afternoon the spacemen had returned to their bus and taken off. The CID men were packed up and the dogs long gone. He'd sent his deputies off to other calls and was preparing to depart himself, the captain of the ship last to disembark.

Elmo sighed and returned to his unit.

As it turned out, Elmo didn't need to make the phone calls to the field office in Birmingham.

He was swinging his department Bronco about when he saw a dark sedan coming up the long drive ahead of a cloud of dust. He cut the engine and stepped out. His day was not done. The sedan came to a stop. Government plates.

A man and woman exited the car, the woman driving. Both wore windbreakers, starched shirts, ties and brogans polished to a mirror finish. No need to flash ID.

"Special Agent Kemp," the woman said and flipped open a leather folder to show her unnecessary photo card. Blonde with auburn hair pulled back like a runner. She would have been attractive if she weren't trying so hard not to be.

"Bill Marquez, FBI," the man said offering a hand to Elmo for a firm shake.

4

A small army of federal agents descended on the Cade Farm.

A camp of buses and trailers was set up in the paddock once it had been cleared. Under the direction of special agent Stacy Kemp, they divided the back field, paddock and woods into a twenty-acre grid to search for evidence.

Their own cadaver dogs failed to get a strike and so ground-penetrating radar was brought in.

Two more bodies were found. Again, they were adult males in a common grave. Oddly, they were buried with the carcass of a dog. All were heavily wrapped in thick-ply plastic sheeting and liberally covered with lime which served to flummox the cadaver dogs. But the plastic sheeting made an excellent reflective surface for the radar device.

The new bodies, largely decayed, provided little evidence with no matches for dental records. The forensic osteopath employed by the bureau gave an educated guess that the men were of a mix of Hispanic and indigenous descent. His shot-in-the-dark guess was that they were either Mexican or Central American. The dog, he offered, was a ridgeback.

Other evidence, suspicious if not actual proof of criminality, was uncovered in the extensive search of the property. Buried weapons, semi-automatic rifles with ammo, were found sealed in airtight containers. Two caches of currency were found. One in a mylar bag concealed in a Maxwell House coffee can and buried next to the foundation of the barn. The other was a fat roll inside a thermos and concealed under the insulation between two beams in the house's attic. The cash total was just south of twenty thousand in fifties and hundreds.

"If that's the cash they forgot," one waggish agent said, "what did they remember to take with them?"

The steel shed was the area that intrigued the team the most though it gave up the fewest secrets. It was obviously built for maximum privacy. Though the presence of a computer station was an enigma as there was no internet connection. The purpose of a set-up like that seemed sinister and the team ached to know what might have been on the missing hard drives.

The house yielded a wealth of prints but told them nothing they didn't already know about the occupants other than the presence of an unidentified minor female.

They'd brought along a pile of folded evidence boxes. There wasn't much to fill them. It was a sad harvest that promised to bear little fruit.

A visit to the local middle school revealed that these unidentified prints belonged to Hope Cade, a girl who was registered at the school as the adopted daughter of Levon Cade. That claim, as well as the attendant documentation proved to be fraudulent. The real identity of Hope Cade remained a mystery, for now.

They put out all the usual bulletins and alerts for law enforcement agencies across the country and Alaska to be on the look-out for Levon, George Martin, Meredith and the mysterious Hope Cade. But, with almost a three-week start on them, the agents' expectation for an early capture were dismal.

"You're our expert on this guy, Bill," Stacy said over sandwiches at Fay's, the only eatery in the nearby podunk town of Colby. They were taking a break from the grid search to clear their heads.

"You looking for some kind of special insight, Stace?" Bill said, stirring his coffee while she dug into her cheeseburger.

"You know him best. You've had the experience. That's why they pulled you off a desk to come down here."

"I almost ran him down in Kansas City. Came close. The guy has all the luck in the world of top of being dangerous. All that and a lot of juice. He skated on a list of federal offenses as long as your arm."

"What qualified him for a special dispensation?"

"Money. What else matters?" Bill smiled bitterly. "He had a pathway to billions in taxable funds. That's all the people who hired us cared about. He was pardoned in exchange for a fat payback."

"That's all over now." Stacy dabbed at the corner of her mouth with a napkin. "Four homicides wash away a lot of good will."

"Turned out there was someone he couldn't make a deal with, I guess."

"What do you think's on those hard drives?"

"My opinion? Those are insurance. Either a way to another cash pile or serious dirt. Cade is a chess player. He's always three steps ahead. It's his natural suspicion honed by years of training."

"Who trained him?"

"The same people who pay our salaries. Cade is one of Uncle Sam's misguided children."

"I was in the Corps," Stacy said, smearing a fry through a puddle of ketchup.

"Now why does that not surprise me?"

She flashed a whisper of a smile and was about to reply when the counter girl approached from behind the counter. The smile she'd offered when she took their orders was gone now.

"Anything else for you?" she said.

"I think we're good," Stacy said. "Could we have the check?"

"I won't take your money," the counter girl said. "I heard you talking about the Cades. I only want you back in your car and out of my sight."

The counter girl turned from them to step back behind the counter to offer refills to a pair of old guys seated there.

"And that, in my 'expert opinion'," Bill said as he pushed away from the table, "is why we'll never catch Levon Cade."

A few thousand man-hours and six months later that prediction held true.

5

He got off the Sun Valley bus in front of the post office. The driver had to come to a full stop to open the cargo bin so Ray could pull out his gear trunk and saddle. He walked through the blue cloud of diesel exhaust to cross the main street to a Quick Stop. He scanned the lot for the man he was to meet and saw no prospects. He pulled a phone from his back pocket. A man called to him from the pump island as he started to send a text.

"Ray Smalls?" the man said as he stepped from the side of a new model Ram.

"Mr. Holman?"

"Naw," the black man said, an open smile on his face as he took the handle of the trunk from Ray. "I'm Wes. Lyle was busy this morning and asked me to come pick you up."

"You a hand too?" Ray said as he heaved his saddle into the bed of the truck.

"No way. Family friend, I guess. I'm no good on a horse." Wesley pulled up a leg of a jeans to reveal a steel prosthetic seated in a sneaker. "I think the leg spooks them."

"I have a cousin rides just fine with one leg," Ray said as he slid the trunk up onto the tailgate with the other man's help. "Doesn't even need help getting astride."

"I guess I'm just not a cowboy." Wes nodded toward the younger man's attire. Well broke-in Stetson, work shirt, jeans and well cared for Larry Mahans that looked like they'd seen some mileage. "But *you* look the part."

"Just workin' clothes," Ray shrugged.

"You need anything from the convenience store?"

"I'm good. Anxious to see where I'll be working."

"It's an hour out and I'm getting a coffee," Wes said and jerked a thumb at the store.

"In that case, I'd kill for a microwave burrito and an ice tea."

"If you don't mind me saying, you look more Indian than cowboy," Wesley said as he drove them from Carey for the state road.

"I'm Pima. Like Ira Hayes. You heard of him?"

"I was Army, but we all heard about Ira Hayes."

"That how you lost the leg?"

"Funny thing is, it's not like I lost it. Damned things still itches and there's no way to scratch it. Did you serve?"

"No, sir. I just turned twenty. There's still time."

"Not sure I'd join up, the way things are now."

"Hm," was all Ray could say to that, not sure what the other man was referring to.

***

Elysium was a fancy name for what turned out to be a humble ranchstead.

To Ray's experienced eye it all looked to be a work

in progress. He could see where the drive going in had a fresh layer of aggregate and new fencing had been put in. The house looked to be freshly whitewashed though the barn could use a shot of paint. What looked like a new travel trailer, a twenty-four footer, sat on concrete hard stand. Parked in the yard before the house was a new Ford pickup, lifted with four-wheel drive, and a Toyota 4Runner. A partly restored El Camino was under a steel carport to one side of the barn. The doors and hood looked to be recently primered.

They cruised along the fence line toward the house. Two girls were unsaddling horses in the paddock where they stopped to watch the Ram pull in. The taller of the two, a girl with shoulder-length hair the color of sand, turned to take a look. The smaller, younger of the pair, held the reins of one of the quarter horses. She was still a kid, ebon hair tied back in a ponytail. But the sandy blonde did a lot for the chaps and high-waisted jeans she wore with a faded USMC T-shirt.

"I know what you're thinking, Hoss," Wesley said without turning from the wheel. "Those are Lyle's girls. The oldest is only sixteen. You get my meaning?"

"You mean there's lots of places to bury bodies out here," Ray said, turning to Wesley with a crooked grin.

"Smart boy." Wesley brought them to a stop next to the Ford.

"The trailer's all yours," Wesley said climbing from the cab. "I'll help you get settled after you meet the boss."

Ray followed the other man across the deep

flagstone veranda into the house and through a great room. The furniture he saw was nothing fancy. Sturdy and serviceable. A couple of framed prints on the walls but no family photographs. There was a TV mounted on the wall between two bookcases crammed with paperbacks and DVDs.

The chugging sound of an engine filled the house. Once they were through and into the back, Ray saw the source. An older guy, gray and a bit chunky, was operating a backhoe while a second man offered directions with hand gestures. They were digging trenches that looked to be a footing for an addition to the house.

Wesley cupped his hands to be heard over the scraping of the bucket in the hardpacked sand. The old man stopped the digging and let the engine idle. The other man turned to regard the newcomers. A tall guy with broad shoulders and light-colored hair trimmed close to the skull. Jeans and Timberlands. The T-shirt he wore allowed Ray to see the raised hash marks of old scars on the man's forearms.

"Lyle Holman," Levon said and took Ray's offered hand. "Let's talk inside."

"You want I should keep going?" the older man in the backhoe seat called.

"Take a break," Levon said and waved him to follow. To Ray he said, "I leave him out here to dig and we'll have a foundation as crooked as a country road."

Inside, Levon guided Ray to the kitchen where he poured himself a cup of coffee from a percolator. He offered Ray a mug but the younger man waved him away with a polite refusal. Wesley took a mug from a hook and poured for himself.

"Bus ride okay?" Levon said, gesturing Ray to a seat at a scarred kitchen table.

"Some dude who wanted to tell me his life story got off in Ogden, Utah. After that it was all right."

"How's your uncle?"

"I haven't seen Uncle Jimmy in a while. He kind of comes and goes since he quit the Border Patrol."

"What's he been doing since?"

"He doesn't talk about it. Says it's the Lord's work."

"He's a good man," Levon said. "Speaks highly of you. That carries a lot of weight with me. I know him from Ranger school. Stand up guy."

"Well, I appreciate the job," Ray said. "And your offer was generous. Getting harder to find work at decent pay. Lot of competition from illegals."

"I need someone who knows what they're doing around a ranch. Help with the horses. And we're gonna put a few head on the grass."

"The grass looks good. What's the water like?"

"Lousy. That's why only a few."

"A hobby farm, then," Ray said and regretted it.

"I guess that's what it is," Levon said without taking offense. "I just want enough steers to qualify for greenbelt. Saves on taxes. Makes me a few bucks."

"And it seems like a waste to not put livestock on all that free government grass."

"That's the kind of thinking we need," Wesley put in.

"I'll need a horse. Maybe two," Ray said and cast his eyes toward the kitchen window. He could see those two girls leading their unsaddled mounts into the barn.

"There's a sale barn in Ketchum in a few days,"

Levon said. "Until then you can ride Charlie, my gelding."

"What'll you ride?" Ray asked.

"I only have a horse because my girls insisted. I don't get that much fun out of it other than seeing them enjoy themselves."

"From what I saw, they look like they know what they're doing," Ray said, and once again, regretted speaking his mind.

"They're good girls," was all his new boss said but there was a greater meaning behind it.

"You're probably worn out from that ride," Wesley stepped in. "I'll show you your new bunk and let you get a shower and a nap if you like."

"Shower sounds good," Ray said, pushing away from the table.

"Good to have you, Ray. Supper's at four," Levon said.

Wesley helped with the trunk, and they carried it into the trailer and set it atop the table in the galley kitchen.

"You mind a word of advice, Ray?" Wesley said, amused.

"Fire away, sir."

"You head down to Carey your first day off and find yourself a regular girl."

"If you don't mind," Ray said nodding. "I'll act on that like scripture."

6

The trailer wasn't brand new, but someone had done a good job of restoring it. New tile and countertops. A new fridge already stocked with a case of Coors and plenty of makings for sandwiches and such. The bathroom had been re-done as well and he noted, with satisfaction, that the commode was hooked to the septic. No emptying honeypots. There was a flatscreen affixed to the dining-cum-living room wall and another in the bedroom. Both had DVD players. No Wi-Fi this far out.

It was a lot better than the tar paper shack Ray lived in on his last job for a big beef grower outside Tucson. Broiled in summer and frozen in winter bunked in with eight other drovers who couldn't decide whether they liked drinking or fighting better so they did both.

Looked like his only worry here was getting fat.

Ray took a long, stinging shower before settling in. With only a towel about his waist, he stowed the contents of his trunk in the drawers and cabinets. Not that he had much. Six work shirts, undies, a new bag of socks, three pairs of jeans and a second pair of working boots. The contents of his shaving kit fit in the medicine cabinet.

That left his tack items in the trunk, bridle and reins and a fine woven blanket handed down by his dad. He'd store them in the barn's tack room along with his saddle. Under the blanket lay a Henry rifle, a Long Ranger, chambered for .308. He installed the extra-large lever on it so he could use it even with mittens on. A 30x scope in a cloth bag lay with it. He stowed them both up in a long overhead cabinet above the eat-in nook. The last things in the trunk were a sheathed bone handle buck knife and a Cactus Hooey calf rope. He set them aside for the following day when work began.

He stretched out on the full-sized bed knowing he was too amped up from the bus ride to do more than stare at the tin ceiling. Curiosity was making him fidgety. This gig seemed too easy, especially for the pay Mr. Holman was offering. He was used to busting his ass for that kind of money. Maybe it was a favor for his uncle. Mr. Holman said he only knew Uncle Jimmy from Ranger school, and his uncle only said that his new employer was a man of his word. This guy didn't owe him anything.

Most probably it was a gentleman rancher who liked the idea of having a hired hand around. Seemed like the only danger Ray was in was being bored to death. The nearest nightlife was down in Carey. That didn't look like much unless he'd missed something on the ride through town.

A sharp rap on the screen door brought him out of a sleep he hadn't realized he'd fallen into. The room was in partial shadow. Sunlight beamed low through the blinds. It was getting on evening.

Chilled, he tightened the still damp towel about his waist and padded to the door on bare feet. He expected it was Mr. Holman or the black man reminding him of supper.

It was the girls.

The older one turned red and lowered her eyes with a simpering smile. The younger one just stared openly at the half naked man standing behind the screen.

"Yeah?" Ray spoke, half ducked behind the door.

"Daddy says supper's ready if you wanted to come in," the older girl said, raising her eyes from beneath lowered brows.

"I'm Nina and this is Jodie," Hope lied for them both while suppressing a giggle.

"Well, it's good to meet you and you tell your father I'll be right in." Ray nodded as he slowly closed the door.

"It's chili night!" the younger one called back as they turned to walk to the house.

He heard them both break into open laughter as he shut the door the remaining way.

***

Chili was the grandfather's specialty and the old man, after introductions, made Ray welcome by asking him to take the cornbread from the oven.

The kitchen was all business without the usual touches a woman brings. Steel countertops and solid wood cabinets painted white. A Wolf gas range and a Subzero fridge you could hang a half steer in. A butcher block table served as the common workspace in the middle of the room.

"Hope it's hot enough for you," Uncle Fern, now Grandpa Holman, said as he diced white onions for garnish.

"I'm sure it's better than anything at my last job, sir." Ray helped himself to a knife from a block and sliced the cornbread into a grid.

"If not, there's Tabasco and a bottle of Texas heat on the table. Help me in with the chili pot."

"Ray's not here to be kitchen help, old man," Levon said as he pushed himself into the long plank table in the vaulted dining room. The girls were already seated and speaking conspiratorially.

"It's all right, sir. Anything to get the food to the table," Ray said. "I haven't eaten since that burrito in the truck."

"Then brace yourself, Ray," Wesley said coming in from the great room at the center of the house. "This chili is strong stuff."

"Not for you, right?" Fern said as he spooned steaming ladles into bowls and handed them around. "Bet Ray was wolfin' down habaneros before he could walk."

"Not exactly, sir." Ray said, accepting a bowl. "Only it sometimes took a half bottle of sriracha to choke down some of the meals at my last job."

The men asked casual questions about Ray's last job. He sensed it was mostly to make conversation, to welcome him. He told them a story he cleaned up for the girls about the time part of a herd he'd been tending broke fence and got into a neighboring commercial vineyard. They ate a few thousand dollars of wine grapes before he and two other guys could round them up. He didn't add the details about the effect the not-quite-ripe grapes had on the cows' digestion.

The meal was good, and filling. By the time he was helping clear the dishes from the table he felt less like a guest and more part of an outfit, small as it was.

"Do you have a girlfriend?" Hope asked as they carried bowls and glasses to the kitchen sink.

"Nina!" Merry said, cheeks darkening.

"Yeah, I do." It was Ray's turn to lie. "I mean, kind of. I met a girl on the bus coming in. She got off in Carey when I did. She gave me her number and we're gonna get together next time I'm in town."

Hope nudged Merry, a smirk on her face. Merry gave her a drop-dead stare.

7

Lew Dollinger was holding up one end of the bar at the Punta Gordo Marriott. It was closing in on last call and he was checking out the talent that remained. He was in that sweet spot. Just drunk enough to fuzz the eye of the beholder but not so drunk that he couldn't ride the pony.

Not much to choose from tonight as the Florida summer was coming to an end. The schoolteachers taking advantage of the cheaper seasonal rates were heading back north. Damn shame as they were easy to separate from the herd. A little older than he'd prefer, hell, sometimes older than him. Didn't matter so long as they didn't mind shacking up with a dog-faced old bastard like himself.

He was watching a redhead eight stools down. She was nursing her third margarita and looking best of breed in skinny jeans and flowered top. Cross-legged with a fuck-me shoe swinging time to the canned music, a dainty gold anklet catching the light with each swing. Had to be a pro, Lew thought. Way too much flash to be alone at this time of the night.

That and the way she was keeping a predatory eye on a booth full of dudes getting loaded on schooners of Heineken. Business types in town for an expo in their matching polo shirts with company logos on the breasts.

A dry well tonight, he sighed to himself. That's the way the biscuit crumbles. He was sober enough for the ride to his rental outside Fort Myers.

A couple times a week, he'd go for a drive up and down the coast. Sarasota, Bradenton, Port Charlotte, Bonita Springs or wherever else there were lonely ladies looking for romance. More times than not, to his surprise, he struck gold. They might be older, fatter or more buck-toothed ugly than he'd care for, but when the lights were low and with the proper dose of Jim Beam, it was all the same in the end. And he never had to pay for a room. Shit, sometimes he'd get breakfast in bed before his fare thee well.

Only this extended vacation of his was going to have to come to an end sometime. He was running low on funds. It was time to get back to work.

Though Lew wasn't sure what form that would take from here on. A dead congressman, all that shit swirling around about kiddie porn along with his own near-death experience caused Lew to take flight from Huntsville to the Gulf coast to make himself scarce.

Congressman Barnes dead by his own hand and the shit storm that hit the news about his ties to trafficking kids out of foster homes was something that wasn't going to die down anytime soon. And somewhere in the investigations and poking around it was for damned sure bagman and fixer Lewis Tyler Dollinger's name was going to come up.

No choirboy by anybody's standards, it gave him a greasy feeling to know he'd been taking money from a baby raper. It made him sick to know that his name was even associated with shit like that. Lew not only drew the line at that sort of thing, but he also failed to understand it all. Much as he liked his carnal pleasures, his taste was plain and simple and restricted to grown women. Most any kind of woman as long as she was over the age of consent and white. Though he'd made exception for the occasional Asian.

Guilty or not, Lew's fortunes were now tied to that fucker Barnes. Sure as shit, none of his former clients would want him anywhere near them because of this new taint. They never minded using a bottom-feeder like him to do their off-the-books dirty work. But accusations, even unproven ones, turned him toxic once kids were mixed in.

He'd have to get serious about finding a new home for himself. Somewhere outside Alabama. A new home and a new clientele for his particular talents.

Those were all the practical business considerations he mulled over most of his waking hours. Underneath of those were memories of his last night in Huntsville. The men that dragged him out of his apartment. The big motherfucker who killed them before dragging Lew out into the sticks only to set him free. The same motherfucker who probably killed his cousin Gage and Gage's buddy Bear. Leastways, neither of them ever came back from that trip to Sugar Run. The motherfucker who was the one who stirred up the shitpot that got all of this mess started.

He made a promise to that man that night. On his

knees and this close to losing his mud, he swore to God, Jesus and on his mother's soul that he'd leave Alabama and never come back.

But a man's got to make a living. Every dog has to do something to earn his daily bone.

Lew cast his eyes along the bar. The redhead was idly picking salt off the rim of her drink with a glass swizzle. Long fingers tipped with posey pink nails guided the stick to lips that gleamed like peach slices. Her smokey eyes narrowed as the booth full of polo shirts slid to their feet and walked to the lobby.

What the hell, Lew thought to himself. Let tomorrow take care of itself manana. A man has a right to spoil himself now and again.

He dropped off his stool and sidled along the bar to take the seat next to her.

"I don't do anal," she said before he could even offer an opening line.

"I am offended, darling," he said, a hand to his chest in mock outrage. "What about me made you assume I'd engage in such?"

"Same thing that told me you don't have five hundred bucks."

"It so happens I can cover the going rate. Though, at this late hour, I have a feeling you'd take three hundred."

She turned to him with a hard look. He beamed at her as he waved the bartender over.

"One more?" Lew said as the bartender joined them.

"Sure. Only put some tequila in it this time, Eric," she said.

"Another Jim Beam for me," Lew said.

She took a phone from a tiny, bejeweled clutch

and sent a quick text. He didn't mind. It gave him time to study her while they waited.

Maybe he'd leave the lights on this time.

They had the elevator to themselves as they rode up to the third floor. They rode as strangers. Damned cameras everywhere these days. Besides, she didn't look like the type to start work until the clock started.

At the room, she slid her card key into the slot and pushed the door open to allow him first entry.

"Wash some of the whiskey stink off you first," she said.

She was resenting the discount he was getting. This was going to be a grudge fuck on her part. Made no difference to him either way. Though, good as she looked, it made him miss the kind of grateful affection he'd come to enjoy from vacationing fourth grade teachers.

He stepped into the room, a suite, in search of the bathroom.

What he found was a tidy little man in a shiny black suit idly channel surfing from the sofa. Accompanying the tidy little man were two very large men who lifted Lew from the carpet like a child.

8

Without a word of introduction, the two linebackers drove Lew to the floor. One held him pinned with a knee in his back and patted him down while the other stood on his outstretched wrists. A quick frisk turned up the Glock in his waistband holster. A more thorough inspection uncovered the hammerless snubby in one cowboy boot and the flick knife in the other. The weapons, his wallet, his phone and key ring all went to the dresser top.

They carried him into the bathroom, ramming the door open with his head. The tidy little man followed. They brought him to the already filled tub and plunged him, head and shoulders, into the cold water.

They let him up gasping only to submerge him once more, then once again. His vision was going red around the edges. He kicked his legs to free them to no use. His calves were locked in the grip of hands the size of bear paws.

Finally, they dropped him on his ass onto the tiles by the tub.

The tidy little man sat atop the toilet lid regarding Lew with an expression of distaste. He wore a highly tailored suit with a black-on-black tie combination with roach-kicker dress shoes polished to a high sheen. Dark eyes watched through tinted lenses as Lew sucked air. Lew noticed the man had lain a bath towel atop the toilet lid. The little pink strip of paper assuring guests that the shitbowl had been sanitized was still in place.

"Levon Cade," the tidy little man said sounding out the syllables. Lee. Vahn. Cay. Duh.

"Fuck," Lew said, spitting a wad of phlegm to the tiles.

"You know this man?" There was a trace of an accent. The tidy little man was Chinese or Vietnamese or some other brand of gook.

"I know about him."

"You have met him, seen him." An accusation not a question. Someone did their homework.

"Once. It didn't go so well."

"He let you live. Explain."

"I been wonderin' about that myself."

"You understand that it is best not to lie to me."

"I'm not a complete idiot," Lew said.

"I am not here to debate the extent of your idiocy, Mr. Dollinger." Mis-tah Dough-ringer. "It is in your interest to be open with me."

"What do want to know?"

"We want to know where Levon Cade is."

"How the fuck should I know that? You know he nearly killed me. For sure killed two of my associations. I don't know his whereabouts and would be pleased-as-shit never to meet him again."

The tidy little man nodded, and the gorillas took

hold of Lew's arms to lift him, boot heels squeaking, from the tiles.

Lew knew this would be the last dunking. Deep down in his lizard brain he knew it.

He fought with an animal fury. He was no longer a man set on tolerating a beatdown. This was a fight for his life. The colors of the room leapt into vivid contrast. His mind and body were taken over by a singular urge to be free. He wriggled. He kicked. He bit. He was a fish on a gaffe.

Somehow, he broke from the grip of the two men. He stumbled back, slick soles slipping on the wet tiles. He met the front of a vanity with a crash and struggled to rise. The big men grabbed him and yanked him to his feet. The veneer of professionalism had vanished. He'd gone and pissed them off.

One of them twisted his right arm behind his back, drawing his hand up between his shoulder blades as he was pressed back against the man's chest. Lew pulled down on an iron cast forearm to keep it from sliding into a chokehold.

"Hold on!" he shrieked. "Hold on one fucking second!"

The tidy little man must have assented as he was dropped to his knees. The two super-sized assholes loomed over him.

"You have something you wish to tell us?" the tidy little fucker said.

One of the goons gripped Lew's head like a basketball to ratchet him around to face the midget seated atop the potty.

"You're looking for him. Can't find him," Lew said, fighting for breath. "I found him once. I can find him again."

"You're suggesting we employ you."

"Welp, you keep killing your sources you're never gonna find squat."

The tidy little man pressed his lips together.

"You're coming up dry everywhere else, am I right?" Lew felt bolder. The gook was all ears. Now who's gaffed, huh? "Why not turn *me* loose?"

"Do you have any leads, Mr. Dollinger?"

"Not at the moment or, swear to God, I'd share 'em with you so's you don't drown me. But I can pick up the trail. Give me a couple weeks."

The tidy little man considered this.

"You can always drown me some other time." This got a spontaneous snort from one of the gorillas.

"I will consider it." The little man rose and exited the room, the man mountains followed without a backward glance. He heard the hotel room door open and close.

Lew sat a moment on the puddled floor until his heart rate returned to something like normal. He staggered to his feet, stripping off boots and his wet clothes and throwing them to the carpet as he crossed the room to the mini-bar.

He downed ten teensy bottles without even reading the labels. Just snapped off the tops and sucked them dry. Rum. Vodka. Gin. Bourbon. Didn't matter. Flopping on the bed in his boxers and socks, he stared at the ceiling, willing the room to stop spinning.

Somehow, he fell asleep, flat on his back atop the covers. He awoke, shivering, at the housekeeper's knock.

"Go the fuck away!" he called as he rose.

He was using the hand dryer on his sodden camp

shirt and khakis when another rap came on the door.

"I said I'm busy!"

"Room service, sir." A female voice through the door.

He wrapped a towel around his waist and answered the door to a smiling Latina pushing a cart laded with covered dishes, a pitcher of OJ and a thermos of coffee.

"I didn't order room service," Lew said. It ain't even my room, he did not add.

"Well, someone did, Mr. Dollinger," she said. "And paid for it too. As well as leaving this for you."

Next to the sweating OJ pitcher lay an unmarked business envelope. The girl rolled the trolley to the middle of the room and departed.

Lew plucked a piece of bacon off the plate of eggs, home fries and biscuits. He slit open the envelope with a thumbnail as he chewed. Inside was a thick wad of hundreds folded into a piece of hotel stationery. There was also a black credit card with his name on it. He rapped it on the dresser's granite top.

Steel.

He unfolded the stationery. Written in neat block lettering were two words.

TWO WEEKS

9

"So, what do you need me to do first, Mr. Holman?" Ray asked.

"I was thinking you'd tell me," Levon said, turning on the spigot to a hose that ran to a cement mixer where Wesley was slitting bags of Sakrete.

"You need help putting up this block?" Ray gestured to the new concrete pad and the stacks of cinderblock set atop it.

"That's not what I hired you for," Levon said, running water into the barrel while Wesley poured mortar mix inside. "I need you to look after the horses and figure out how we can put some livestock on the grass. What we'll need and who we'll see about it."

"I can do that. I can do fencing too. You're gonna need something stouter than that split rail if you want to hold cows penned."

"That's the kind of stuff I need done. Mending fences, riding herd, shoeing horses. Cowboy work."

"Ranch hand, more like," Ray shrugged. "I can do all of that but if you need more than a thrown shoe replaced or some trimming, you're gonna need a real farrier."

"A who-ier?" Wesley asked.

"A blacksmith," Levon put in. "I know that much. How do we find one? A good one?"

"I'd ask around the sale barn when we go to pick out those horses. You can get on their regular route."

"Thanks for being honest," Levon said. "About not being a pro at shoeing."

"Only fair. Most horsemen don't do their own iron other than temporary repairs. Too much to consider and too easy to hobble a horse by screwing it up. It's best left to guys who know what they're doing."

"Then you spend the day looking over the property and getting ideas for where to put the cattle," Levon said, as he dug in a tool bag for trowels and a level. "Sale barn's tomorrow so make it a half day and get some sleep. It's a long drive to Ketchum."

"Yes, sir," Ray said and stepped over the footing ditch to make his way around the house.

"Looks like you hired the right man," Wesley said as he started up the mixer motor.

"He'll do," Levon said.

***

"You like Ray," Hope said.

"Sure, don't you?" Merry said from where she stood at the kitchen door.

"I mean really like him," Hope said, beaming as she put breakfast plates in the dishwasher. "Liiiiiiiiike him."

"Not like that. What do you think? I'm gonna fall in love with *any* boy?" Merry watched Ray step over the footing to make his way through the trees around the side of the house.

"You mean the *only* boy."

"Exactly, Hopey. He's the only boy near my age for twenty miles around. That's not enough reason to get all googly over him."

"He's very nice."

"He seems that way."

"He's handsome."

"You know," Merry said, scooping up silverware from the table, "I'm starting to be sorry I taught you English."

"And he has a girlfriend already." Hope took the forks and spoons from her to place them in the silverware basket.

"Hm. Maybe," Merry said.

"Maybe she'll dump him."

"Why are you so interested in pushing us together?" Merry said, filling the detergent bin on the dishwasher door.

"We don't have TV," Hope said, sadly.

10

Selling the Caddy took a piece of his soul with it.

It was like a friend. His Batmobile. He realized he had a longer relationship with that car than with any human being in his life. He had promised himself he'd be buried in it one day.

That was before the events in Punta Gordo. Now he was more likely to be tossed in a landfill packed in separate trash bags.

It wasn't like Lew Dollinger had much of a choice. If he was going to find Cade it meant starting at the beginning of the trail. That meant going back to Alabama. And he for damned sure couldn't do that in Baby, his chrome-encrusted, sky blue El Dorado.

He traded her in at a dealership in Tampa for a 2011 Tundra. The deal cost him an additional five grand; severely gouging what was left of his ever-shrinking kitty. He made the salesman swear that Baby wouldn't be sold for parts. The salesman gave his solemn word, agreeing that chopping a creampuff like that would be a sin before God and man.

Changing rides wasn't enough. He stopped in a

Walgreen's and picked up a bottle of Lady Clairol. In the bathroom sink of a Budget Inn in Ocala he dyed his hair. He had to take special care as the hair on top was fine and sparse and he didn't want to stain his scalp. He'd begun a beard at the start of his enforced vacation and combed dye into that as well. It helped alter the shape of his face, but he was unhappy with the shade. The girl on the box sported a silky auburn do. His results came out redder than he liked making his already pale complexion appear even whiter. A spray tan applied during his stay at a Motel 8 in Gainesville left him looking like an Amish Donald Trump. At least he didn't look like himself. He'd picked up a Gators ballcap to complete his disguise.

The long ride up through central Florida, with a country oldies station on the radio for company, left him time to think on how best to proceed. He'd visit the Cade place first, taking 231 off Florida 10 to drive up the eastern half of Alabama and thus avoid his old haunts of Birmingham and Huntsville. A snoop around to see if he could find any hints as to where Cade had run to. It was probably pointless. The tidy little man and whoever he was working for had probably done a thorough toss. But Lew needed a place to start, needed to get more of a sense of his quarry.

He pulled off the highway for lunch at a Cracker Barrel and lingered over a chicken pot pie and fries. That two-week deadline was serious. Find Cade in two weeks, now twelve days, or go on the run from the gook and his two bodybuilders. A no-shit lifetime run.

Still, he was not anxious to cross over into Bama.

He had a sense there was trouble there, more trouble than he was taking into account. That sense had saved his ass a time or three and he learned to pay attention to it. There had to be a way to take a peek down the road before he crossed the state line.

There was a public library in the poky little town of Quincy just west of Tallahassee. Lew found himself a computer terminal and logged on. Just for the sheer hell of it he Googled "Levon Cade" and was surprised when a long string of news articles popped up. Most of them local, state papers. *The Tuscaloosa News. The Dothan Eagle. The Decatur Daily. The Huntsville Times.* All starting about six months back.

The stories were the same with varying degrees of vague details. Four bodies were found on the Cade property and homicide was the cause of each. The FBI and the staties were all over and a nationwide search for Levon and George Martin Cade was set in motion. Persons of interest. The articles began to peter out over the ensuing weeks leaving one last single column piece in the Huntsville paper three months back.

Details were scarce but two of the victims, both locals, were identified. Lew took down their names in his pad. The two other bodies were not identified. All had been buried on the property.

The only other name mentioned was Meredith Cade, Levon's daughter. She was missing along with her father and uncle. No mention of that wild-ass nigger he'd run into up at Sugar Run. The whole clan was on the run for parts unknown.

At near six months cold, there'd be no surveillance remaining on the Cade place. He'd been a deputy himself in another life and had experience with feds a time or two. Lazy pencil pushing fuckers more concerned with their careers than being any kind of real cop. Levon Cade would be near the bottom of their pile of priorities.

Still, he'd need to tread with caution. Lew Dollinger was a man who liked to hedge his bets, an ace up his sleeve and a peek at the other fella's hand. Further up Florida Ten he pulled off at Mariana and found an Office Max where he had them make him up a hundred business cards for Art Blodgett to match the name on the phony driver's license he was traveling under. According to the cream-colored cards, Blodgett was a freelance insurance agent. The card featured the number to one of his burner phones and a fax number and email address he'd made up. A chirpy little gal at the Office Max suggested including the logos of some of the companies he did business with and so tiny little images of the symbols for Farmers, All-State and Geico ran across the top margin giving it a snappy, professional appearance.

Armed with his new look and a boring but believable excuse for asking nosey questions, Lew powered the Tundra west to turn north toward Dothan on the other side of the Alabama line.

11

Early morning, the Ram followed the tunnel cut in the gloom by its high beams. The rising sun was creating a creamy wisp in the iron sky where the dawn light struck the snow atop the peaks in the far distance.

The girls pestered Ray Smalls with questions about his family and cowboying and life on a reservation for the first forty-five minutes of the two-hour drive to Ketchum. Mostly they asked about his girlfriend in Carey.

"What's her name?" Hope asked.

"Carrie."

"Her name is Carrie, and she lives in Carey?" Merry asked.

"I think her folks named her after the town. Carrie Ann."

"How long have her folks lived there?" Merry asked.

"What color is her hair?" Hope asked simultaneously.

"She didn't say a lot about them, and I guess you'd

say she was kind of a dirty blonde."

"Dirty blonde?" Hope canted her head, uncomprehending.

"You said you talked on the bus for hours." Merry again.

"Not about family."

"Then what did you talk about?" Merry once more.

"Stuff we like. Movies we've seen. Music. You know."

"What's her favorite music?" Merry leaned between the two seats for the answer.

"Oh, Cowboy Junkies. Whiskeytown. Cat Power. Stuff like that."

"I've never heard of them," Merry said.

"They're alt country. You don't hear them much on the radio." They were acts he liked, and he hoped the subject might change to music.

No such luck.

"Where are you going on your first date?" This from Hope.

"You know what, ladies?" Levon broke in from behind the wheel of the Ram. "You need to let Ray up for air."

Ray sighed in relief. He was running out of lies. He turned to Merry.

"You know, we just passed a cell tower. I bet you girls have some bars by now."

The phones came out and the girls sank back into the backseat, thumbs flying.

"We won't hear from them again," Levon said.

Ray looked out at the land stretching away either side of the two-lane they'd been on since they left the ranch. The mountains ahead never seemed to get any nearer as they drove. He marked the indigo blue peaks capped with white against the top of the windshield. The truck was cruising at 70 and, if anything, the range looked like it was getting farther away with every mile.

"Awful generous of you buying me a horse, Mr. Holman," he said to break the long silence.

"You need a ride. You had a company horse before?" Levon said, eyes ahead on the empty road.

"A whole remuda. I had my favorites. Haven't owned a horse since I left the family place. Do you ride much, Mr. Holman?"

"I can. I do. Mostly to keep the girls company."

"The animals you have are just fine. You have a good eye."

"Trust me, Ray, I got lucky. I assume you know the kind of mount you want best."

"A two-year old. Quarter horse. Cow pony. I know what to look for and I know how to haggle."

"I want to pick up two for you. No sense straining a single mount."

"Just how hard are you planning on working me, sir?" Ray smiled.

"Not you I'm worried about. It's the horses." Levon glanced at him, eyes betraying amusement.

The dusty two-lane merged with a surface road that led eventually to 75 North. The highway ran straight as a string toward the wall of gray rock spread along the horizon from end to end. The peaks had climbed to within a hair of the top of the windshield while they talked. The road appeared to be on a collision course with the Rockies. As it made its way between mountains, it turned from two lanes to three, two heading north and one south. The rocks rose up either side of them leaving a narrow gap lined with homes and businesses for much of its length.

By the time they reached Ketchum there was actual traffic. All of it led to the sale barn, a collection of steel hangars surrounded by ten acres of parking with nearly every space taken. Levon pulled the truck and horse trailer to a spot on the grass along a fence line. The girls exploded from the truck to run ahead.

"Horses," was all Levon said.

"Cows too," Ray said, sniffing the air.

By nine in the morning Ray made his first choices. Stock was going fast all around without much room for dickering. Ray settled on a red dun and a buckskin with black stockings. Both working horses, both geldings, not the racing variety. Stocky, well-muscled with an easy demeanor. When it came time to pay up, Levon told Ray to begin the registry paperwork.

"They'll need your ID, sir," Ray said.

"Register them both in your name."

"That's not how it works, sir. They're not my horses," Ray said.

"They are now," Levon said, peeling a last hundred off a fat wad of bills and placing it atop the stack of bills on the dealer's table.

"I'm not sure I can accept that, Mr. Holman. You're paying some steep prices here."

"Think of it as a Christmas bonus three months in advance."

The girls rejoined them at the trailer with food truck egg and sausage sandwiches and coffee.

"I saw a pig this big," Hope said, stretching out her

arms as far as they would reach.

Levon and Ray loaded and secured the new horses in the trailer before removing their gloves for a casual picnic on the Ram's tailgate.

"They loaded well," Levon said.

"Always a good sign," Ray agreed.

"You picked out names yet?" Merry said.

"They already *have* names," Ray said, waving the folded sheaf of sale papers. The registry from the AQHA would come in the mail in a few weeks.

Merry took the bills of sale and examined them.

"Billy Pete? Windy Gale? What kind of names are those for a horse?"

"The breeders come up with them. I sure hope the buck isn't windy," Ray said, grinning through a cheek full of hash browns and biscuit.

"We need to give them better names," Merry said with Hope nodding.

"Be my guest," Ray said. "As long as it's nothing sissy."

By the time they were off the highway and on Buttercup Road for home, the girls had dubbed the dun Flame and the buckskin Tommy.

12

Lew breathed easier when he saw the county auction sign at the end of the Cade driveway.

The sign declared that the lot, house, barn, and contents were going on the block in thirty days down at the county seat. Sold for back taxes.

That meant there'd be lots of lookie-loos and curious neighbors showing up the rest of the month. He'd just be one more.

All was quiet at the end of the drive. There was still police tape in place though most of it was faded and hanging limp where it had been torn away from the entrances to the house, barn and a metal shed.

He took pictures with his phone as he walked the house. There were a few papers scattered on the floor. Old utility bills and magazines. A pair of bookcases packed with old paperbacks and Gun Digests. The feds would have taken the rest and filed it away like squirrels. No computers anywhere. Either the Cades or the feds have taken them. Dishes, glasses and cookware still in the kitchen.

There were some floorboards pulled up and a gun safe stood open empty as a tomb. The house had been gone over. First by the Cades and then by the federales. He checked the metal shed. It was a workshop with power tools on stands or neatly hung on the walls along with rows of organizers for hardware. Some kind of computer workstation and an empty roller cart that once held a printer.

The government boys took a special interest in this place. Most of the surfaces from eye level to below were still greasy with fingerprint powder. Nothing to see so Lew moved on to the barn.

There were stalls open and the smell of horse piss gone ripe. They'd even taken the horses with them. He exited the barn and stood on the gravel of the yard to scan the surrounding trees looking for inspiration.

This place was a wash. What the Cades had not carted off, the feds had scooped up. The place was a dead end. This fucker knew how to bug out and left jack dick behind to point to what direction he'd gone. If the FBI had gone cold on him then it was near to a lost cause.

Defeated, Lew slid behind the wheel of the Tundra and swung it around to point it back toward the road. He followed the rutted drive past the fence line that ran down one side of the paddock. The grass had grown high with no animals to graze on it.

He stood on the brakes to bring the truck to a juddering halt.

The horses.

***

The library in Haley had three terminals and all three were busy. Lew flipped through some magazines he'd pulled off the rack and watched the three old bastards hunched over the keyboards. One of them, some lardass in stretch shorts, finally pushed his chair back and waddled off. Lew slid into his seat and tapped the keyboard to clear the screen.

"That's Kenny's place," the senior next to him said.

"What'd you say?" Lew replied, eyes on the screen and hand guiding the mouse.

"Kenny had that machine," the ancient shit-bird said. "He only got up to use the men's."

"Old as he is, I'll be long gone before he's drained his pecker," Lew said without turning from the keyboard where he was hunting and pecking.

The old man huffed and turned back to his game of hold 'em.

Lew googled about horse registries. He'd dealt with enough stolen livestock back in his deputy days to know that every horse had papers and a history. Some of them had more documentation than most people do. There was big money in horseflesh and the people who dealt in it wanted guarantees. It would be a lot harder to change a nag's name and pedigree than coming up with phony ID for a person. Chances are, Cade wouldn't even have bothered.

Every site, PHR, USDF and hobby sites, told him the same story. The registry papers on any horse in the United States was a matter of public record. All transparent and on the up and up. The only stumbling block was that, to start a search, you needed each horse's name. And where the hell was he going to find that?

He searched his memory, and he had a keen one, thinking of the Cade barn. There were no names over the stalls. Not even on the feed buckets that were left behind. And all the tack, bridles and saddles and the rest had gone wherever the animals had gone.

"Shit fuck," Lew said and tossed the mouse to the tabletop.

"Language, son," the old prune next to him hissed. "This is a library."

"You know, you're a pain in the ass, old man," Lew said, regarding the stick of a man, neck humped by scoliosis.

"We had guys like you back in the army," the old man said through clenched dentures. "Took 'em behind the barracks and kicked their asses."

"You in World War Two, grandad?" He looked to Lew to be old enough to be in both world wars.

"Guadalcanal."

"That against Nazis or Japs?"

"Japs. And if I was the man now I was then I'd kick *your* ass."

"I like you, granddad," Lew said smiling as he stood to leave. "Now, I'm gonna head back to my Japanese car and leave you to wonder who won your war."

13

Flame and Tommy were released to graze and meet their new corral mates.

Tricky Dick, the Abyssinian goat who'd adopted Fern Cade, bleated from the barn where he was tethered, to let the new horses mingle without his interference.

Everyone, Uncle Fern included, took a place along the fence to watch the ages-old ritual of horses getting to know one another. Rascal, Fern's Jack Russell terrier, lay with his snout under the bottom pole of the fence. Bella, the bluetick hound had little interest in horses and continued her nap in the sun at the foot of the veranda steps.

Merry and Hope's quarter horses, Dusty and Felicia respectively, stood at the far end of the field, ears up and eyes on the two strangers munching flakes of alfalfa. Levon's horse, a dappled gelding named Charlie, seemed particularly interested, pawing up dust with one hoof.

It was Dusty, Merry's nutmeg colored mare, who made the first intro, cantering close to the new pair to stand with her tail swinging and nostrils flared.

Felicia, named for Hope's favorite TV character, followed but kept more distance. Only too-cool-for-school Charlie remained four acres away pretending nothing new had happened. There was a nip and bit of bucking but soon the mares and the new arrivals were grazing together. Charlie, the largest of the animals, would assert his dominance over the next few days and all would settle down.

Ray went to the barn to fill the water and feed buckets for his mounts. He was scooping sweet feed from a battered, defunct chest freezer when Levon entered to join him.

"The girls can do that when they muck the stalls," Levon said.

"Cowboys muck their own stalls, Mr. Holman."

"The girls muck out Charlie's stall. That's my horse."

"You ain't a cowboy."

"I came in to tell you that you can have one of the trucks if you wanted to run into town to see that girl," Levon said.

"There's no girl, sir. That was a little lie."

"Can you tell me why you did that?"

"It was at Mr. Ruskin's suggestion."

"Wes told you to say that?"

Ray nodded and dropped the scoop back into the feed bin. They could hear the girls laughing outside.

"I see," Levon said.

"No offense meant, sir."

"None taken. But the offer still stands. Maybe you want to drive into Carey and *find* a girl."

"Maybe when the weekend comes. It's been a long day and I'm all out of conversation."

"We'll talk more in the morning," Levon said and left him to prepare his new mounts' new home.

14

Lew drove along yet another holler looking for Riverstone Veterinary. There was a couple dozen animal doctors in this backwoods county. Near three times as many as there were clinics for human beings. These hillbillies cared more for their critters than they ever could for themselves or their kin.

Only three of the vets dealt in larger animals and this Riverstone was the last one he had to check out. Stood to reason Cade had a doctor looking after his stock and it was most likely someone within an easy drive of his place.

The business sat on a farmette with a stable building twice the size of the house. Some horses grazed on the thirty or so acres of fenced-in grass. They looked up as he drove past and parked between a Kia sedan and a mid-sized pick-up pulled up to the house.

He climbed onto the porch and gave the bell a good long push. His ear pressed to the frosted pane at the center of the door, he could hear movement within. He pressed the bell again.

The door was jerked open, and a young girl stood blinking at him. She had the wide-eyed look of a fawn stepping into a shaft of sunlight. Face flushed, a few strands of her hair were plastered to her forehead with sweat despite the frostiness of the AC-chilled air escaping around her.

"Yes?" she said, her initial surprise turning to impatience.

"I'm with the Downhome Insurance agency and I had a question about one of your clients," Lew said, a mirthless smile creasing his face. "Or, I should say, one of your daddy's clients."

"You mean the vet's? That's my mother's business."

"Well, is your mother at home?" Lew craned his neck to look past the girl into the house. He saw movement there, a shadow crossing against the light coming from the windows at the back of the house. A male shadow.

"She's on a call out on Corinth Pike. She won't be home till dark."

I just bet she won't, Lew thought to himself and fought down the urge to offer this little sweetheart a knowing wink.

"Well, all's I had was a few questions," Lew said, presenting one of his phony cards. "Maybe you know something."

"Not sure I can help you." She took the card but began to shoulder the door closed.

"Maybe your little friend in there might be able to help me," Lew said, gripping the edge of the door. "I drove a long way."

The girl shrugged by way of reply, eyes hard on him.

"My company wrote a policy on some horses that

your mama may have treated a time or two," Lew said. "The policy is coming up due and we haven't been able to contact the owners."

"Maybe I know them. What's their name?"

"Cade. Levon Cade."

"Oh, *him*," the girl said, her lips twisted as though she might spit. "We haven't seen him in a long time."

"We know they've relocated. We're concerned that the horses will be without coverage."

"Yeah. They moved kinda sudden."

"I'd like to confirm that this is the same owner. Do you recall the names of any of their horses?"

"Sure. There's Montana, a quarterhorse. And Bravo, a gelding. And Penny, that's their pony."

"And has your mother had any further contact with any of the Cades?" Lew was busy making note of the horse's names.

"Naw. They just took off. Barely said goodbye."

"That's very helpful, miss," Lew said, pocketing the notebook. "I'll be able to look up the horses' registries to find my clients."

"Won't do you much good," she said, bringing him to a stop halfway down the porch steps. "The horses are here, registered in my mother's name."

"They're here? The horses, you mean?"

"Levon signed them over to my mother before he left. He wanted to *give* them to her, but she made him sign a bill of sale for a dollar each."

"A dollar each?"

"I told her she oughta sell 'em. She won't though."

"Why not?"

"She keeps thinking he'll come back sometime. Mr. Cade, I mean."

"And you don't think he will."

"I'm *praying* he won't. You want to see the horses?"

"No. That won't be needed." Lew thought, *fuck* no.

He turned to walk to his truck. The girl watched him a while through the ajar door before closing it to return inside.

A dead end. A cold trail. He'd blown two days of his allotted fourteen on a snipe hunt. He sat behind the wheel, hands fisted and searched for a new avenue to the man he hunted. He needed some kind of connection that would draw a straight line from these hills to wherever Cade was holed up.

Selling three horses with papers for less than a pack of cigarettes. Was that the kind of hurry he was in? The girl said he was willing to give them away, give them to her mama. Why not just let them run free? Or leave them? Was it the horses he cared about or the animal doctor? Whatever it all meant it described a degree of trust between the girl's mama and Cade. From the bitter reaction of the girl, maybe it was more than that.

He backed from between the parked cars to drive out of the stable yard, lost in his thoughts as he gained the county road to head into Haley for the motel room he had here. There was something there for sure, something Cade left behind. Some unfinished business. An angle.

Patty Loveless came on the radio and he tapped time with his fingerprints on the steering wheel as he drove north. He could spend the remainder of one of his precious days mulling the best way forward. Tomorrow was another day and he had one more idea he wanted to explore.

15

"What do you know about cattle, Mr. Holman?" Ray said as he poured himself a thermos full of coffee.

"Nothing. That's what I hired you for," Levon sat at the kitchen table with a few *Cattleman* magazines he'd picked up along with a couple of livestock catalogs.

"Well, those are no good," Ray said. "It's all done online now. All the information in those magazines is old before you get it."

"Internet connection's zero out here," Fern said, setting down a plate of eggs and toast before taking a seat himself.

"You saw it. The girls have to drive halfway to Ketchum or Bellevue to get a signal," Levon said.

"Starlink's in beta now," Ray said, capping his thermos.

Both men looked at him uncomprehending.

"It's Elon Musk's satellite internet. You buy some hardware and get all the access you want for a hundred a month."

"Well, shit," Fern said.

"I read more than feed bags. You thinking of raising beef for sale?"

"That's what I thought. Get this place green belted," Levon said.

"The grass isn't rich here, but you have a lot of it," Ray said. "You could get a dozen calves to start. Sell 'em in the spring. That is if your girls don't name them all."

"What about breeding?"

"That's a more expensive proposition, sir. I can wrangle them and care for them, but siring calves is more for experts."

"I thought that just come natural," Fern huffed.

"There's more science to it than that. At least if you're looking to make a name for yourself, sir."

"I don't want a brand," Levon said. "Just a hobby farm, like you said."

"Do you know any of your neighbors? One of them might give you a good price on a couple calves to get your started."

"I haven't really met any. There's the Bingham's five miles south and the Tollhouse ranch over at the Jerome cut-off."

"An excuse to meet them and talk cows," Ray said. "Always good to know the ranches nearest you. People rely on each out here more than in the east. You might need them sometime. Or they'll need you."

"As long as you come along with me so my good neighbors don't make me pay through the nose," Levon said.

"Maybe we could get one dairy cow," Fern said, gesturing with a corner of toast at Ray. "My pa used to have one we called our ice cream cow. Levon loved that cow when he was a boy."

Ray watched as his boss shot the old man a quick look. The old man's smile faded, and he bent back to his eggs. Something happened there. Maybe Levon was a relative who passed. Or family history. Some wounds never heal. None of his business.

"Where you off to today?" Levon said, not looking up from his coffee.

"Unless you have a specific job for me, I thought I'd ride a circle around the property and up on the range land. I'd like to get to know the place."

"I'll leave you to it, Ray. Take one of the radios in case you run into trouble."

Ray picked up a Motorola from a charging station next to the microwave before heading out for the barn. He saddled Flame and led him into the yard before mounting. He rode past the girls reading on the back porch. Wesley was already at work, down in the footing trench, laying a first course of cinder block for the new addition. He'd told Ray he had an engineering background.

He rode out through the tall grass, setting the direction but letting the horse set the pace. The land looked flat as a pancake, but he knew that was a deception. The grass tended to level everything out. Concealed beneath the wavering stalks would be slopes and gullies and washes. This land needed livestock on it to tame it, bring it down where you could see its true face. He headed to the northeast where Mr. Holman told him there was a sometimes water source. It would be up to him to determine their water needs and how many animals this land would support without running a water line out to the herd.

It was the kind of problem he enjoyed solving. And, even more than the generosity, Ray appreciated the faith Mr. Holman showed in him. It was almost like he was his own boss.

That left him to wonder again, and a cowboy spent a lot of his days wondering. What did his Uncle Jimmy mean to this man? And what did this man mean to Jimmy Smalls? It went way past being in basic together. You don't take on an army buddy's nephew like this and treat him like family based on only that. What did the Holmans know about him except his uncle's word that he was a hard worker?

On top of that, what did he know about them? Mr. Holman was in the army and said something about selling a contractor business in Louisiana. He was pretty young to be retired. And Mr. Ruskin was Army too, but he got a sense, from hearing them talk to each other, that they didn't serve together. Maybe they became friends when Mr. Holman was in construction.

They weren't a couple, that was for sure. Wes's meticulously archived collection of vintage Playboys attested to that. No one would go to that much trouble to stay closeted these days especially since they all lived out here like preppers.

And Mr. Holman had been married until he was widowed. Jodie was as obviously his own blood as Nina was obviously adopted. Must be a lonely life, way out here raising two girls on his own.

Ray sniffed at these thoughts. And here I am, on my own since I was sixteen, he thought. The original lonesome Indian, feeling sorry for a guy who's got enough money to start up a ranch with cash.

He heeled Flame to a canter, feeling the wind on

his face and the easy, graceful power of the animal under him as they made their way down a gentle slope. Ray rode out into the endless land, riding across banded shadows cast by tattered clouds crossing the morning sky.

At the foot of the slope, he found the dry wash Mr. Holman had told him about. It was a gully carved across the lower ground by infrequent rains rather than a natural course for snowmelt from the far-off peaks. An unreliable water source that meant there could be no serious number of livestock placed on the land without a serious investment in a reservoir of collection tanks.

He guided the horse down the bank and across the sandy floor of the wash to ride over the next ridgeline.

Five miles off of the Holman back property line Ray came on an old fire road that cut east-west toward the state road twenty miles in that direction. Probably cut through here by either the government or some cattleman's association long ago. Crushed aggregate made a chalk line through the feed grass. The grading followed roughly the same course into the crotch between low hills as the dry wash did. It was still serviceable but poorly maintained, with grass encroaching on either shoulder.

He dismounted and walked the horse along the road surface awhile. There were fresh tracks in the dirt either side where some ATVs or dirt bikes had crossed since the last rain. He crouched to look at the soil and found animal tracks. Coyote. Prairie chicken. Wild turkey. No deer, sadly. Maybe closer to winter there'd be bigger game.

Ray re-saddled and rode Flame back south for the

ranch on a course to the east of the one he took out. He came upon broken ground cut by swales choked with bramble and berry bushes. Doves scattered up out of the brush as he rode along the rim of one of the depressions. He made note of the place as a good spot to scare up small game. He might have to buy a shotgun with his first check.

Down in the tangles of thorn at the mouth of a swale he could see a flash of something white. He ground-reined the gelding to pull away some dried branches to uncover the hood of a car. A few more clumps of cover revealed the front end of a car that had been shrink wrapped in heavy plastic like they do boats for winter storage. Something scattered back deeper into the depression as he pulled away the camouflage. Rabbits, most likely.

The wheels were off the car and the whole waterproofed package rested up on concrete blocks. The cover material had been spray painted over in stripes of brown and green paint to help conceal it. A strip of paint had been worn away where branches rubbed against the roof in the wind. Despite the thickness of the resin wrap, Ray could tell the car was an older model Ford Mustang by the distinctive shape of the hood and front grill.

He replaced the brambles atop the car and remounted.

All the way back to the ranch, he debated with himself whether or not to mention his find. In the end he decided to keep it to himself. None of his business.

16

Another day. Another holler. Another bust-ass drive up another rutted dogleg of a private road.

Lew was glad of the Tundra. His Caddy would have bottomed out on a piece-of-shit track like this one. A good mile from the county road to the Taggart place after spending the past two hours driving up one goatpath after another to ask directions. These hillbillies liked their privacy. No names on the mailboxes. Not even address numbers. And, from the reluctance of the folks he questioned, Lew had a sense that no one was all that eager to share the whereabouts of their neighbor.

No wonder, Lew thought, as he jigged to the right to avoid driving his left wheels into a canyon-sized rut. He'd done his homework on these Taggarts, the public records anyway. There was a shit-pile of them registered with addresses in the county including the one he was approaching. They had a long history of run-ins with the law. A whole clan of felons. Getting arrested was like a rite of passage for them with dozens of arrests for assault, grand theft, criminal trespass, selling unlicensed hooch, firearms violations and even more citations for moving violations, DWIs and speeding. Visiting day at Bullock must be like a family reunion.

He rounded a thick clump of old oaks fringed with sumac to find a collection of steel-roofed buildings. A cacophony of barking dogs rose up as he came in sight of a cyclone fenced dog run that ran behind a kennel building. A few dogs ran loose, big mongrels that trotted toward his approaching truck, silent and heads lowered. They were some kind of mix of ridgeback and mastiff with maybe some hyena DNA mixed in. They circled his slowing truck, eyes brimming with cold menace. Lew pulled to a stop before a long, rambling house sheltered under spreading elms.

The dogs glared at him from the gravel yard. One leapt atop the hood, nails clacking on the steel, to study him with closer scrutiny. Lew pressed down on the horn for a long toot. The dog atop the hood pawed the windshield with a sonorous growl from deep in its chest.

While waiting for a response, Lew looked around the yard between the house and a collection of sheds painted in various colors, all peeling.

What these folks didn't spend on home improvements, they splashed on luxury vehicles, hoopy style. There were three trucks, all Chevys lifted on fat knobby tires to just shy of monster truck status. All sported high-gloss paint jobs waxed to a mirror shine. One, a big Yukon, had a custom Confederate stars and stripes professionally painted on its hood. There was a big-ass Unimog with a flat bed that was all painted in camo colors.

Incongruously, a forest green Range Rover, dainty by comparison, was parked closest to the main house.

There were a couple of trailered bass boats under tarps as well as six or more ATVs parked under a sagging carport.

He gave the horn two more toots. The beast crouching on his hood showed more teeth, ears pinned back. Lew sat weighing his options, determining the best approach.

Someone came out of one of the sheds to holler at the dogs. A big bastard in cut-offs and cowboy boots. Six foot or more and heavy with prison yard muscle. An ornate Celtic cross wrapped in loops of barbed wire was inked on his right breast, a curved dagger dripping blood to the left. He gave the dogs a kick to scatter them as he came closer to the Tundra. With one hand in the collar, he tore the dog off Lew's hood to send it tumbling across the yard. Lew rolled his window down an inch to be heard.

"You lost?" the big bastard said.

"Not if this is the Taggarts'," Lew said, holding his old deputy badge and ID against the window glass. He was careful to position his thumb over the part of the ID card that identified him as from Perry County once upon a time.

"You all by yourself?" The big bastard scanned the trees about looking for deputies or SWAT or ninja turtles.

"Just me myself and I." Lew offered what he hoped was a reassuring smile.

"You got more balls than sense, Sheriff."

"I only want to ask a few questions. Maybe it's your daddy I need to talk to. Roland Taggart?"

"Questions about what?" The big bastard spat a

stream of chaw onto the glass before Lew's face.

"About who. Fella named Levon Cade."

"Pa!" the big bastard roared toward the house.

***

Lew took an offered seat in a slat-back chair on the porch of the house. Rolly Taggart settled into a cushioned lounger and lit up a Marlboro. The big bastard, the 'baby of the clan' as it turned out, took a seat on a porch step to throw a tennis ball for the mongrel who'd scratched hell out of the Tundra's hood.

"You don't mind settin' on the porch? Cooler here than inside."

"Suits me," Lew shrugged. Taggart wouldn't let a lawman through his door without a warrant and a small army of armed cops to back it up.

"Loretta's bringin' sweet tea," Taggart said. "Unless you'd rather have coffee."

"Tea's fine." Lew removed his shades and fixed a grin on his face. "Though I'd not turn down a slash of some of your best."

"I got no idea what you're talkin' about," Taggart said. "'Sides, ain't you on duty?"

"I heard you brew some ass-kickin' white liquor."

"You heard right. Once upon a time. I'm outta that line these days." Taggart twirled a ring on his finger as he spoke. Fat gold band with a red stone the size of a pinky nail.

"Might I ask what area of business occupies your time these days, sir?"

"Got a licensed haulin' business and we do some concrete and gravel work 'round the county."

A woman shouldered the screen door open to

set down a tray with some tall glasses and a pitcher atop a picnic table. She was one of those mountain gals who'd kept her shape despite the years. Coppery hair tied back with a bandana, going gray around the temples. Her eyes were hard as anthracite regarding Lew through tendrils of smoke from the cigarette clamped between her thin lips.

Two kinds of women up here, Lew thought as she poured the glasses full, those that made their own way and those who took the government check. Those that kept their pride kept their figures. Those who took Uncle Sugar's handouts grew fat as hogs. Just the way it was up in here.

"Thank you, ma'am," Lew said, lifting the glass tinkling with ice. "Nothin' better on a day like this one."

She rewarded him with a sneer before tucking the tray under her arm and retreating back into the house.

"Loretta's daddy was killed by sheriffs down Five Points when she was just a girl," Rolly said after the screen door slammed shut like a pistol shot with enough force to set the springs singing.

"That can be tough on a child," Lew said with as much sympathy as he could fake.

"You mentioned Levon Cade," Rolly said.

"Indeed, I did, sir. I've been tasked with finding his ass and I was hoping you might have something to share."

"So, Struthers decided to get off his fat ass?"

"He did just that." Lew had seen the name of the county sheriff on the police reports he'd managed to get a look at. "He put me, the old coon dog, on Cade's trail."

"I know most of the lawmen in county." Rolly stubbed out his butt in a glass ashtray and lit another with a kitchen match. "I've never seen you before."

"That's because I've been re-assigned from down Perry County," Lew said, mixing a pinch of truth into his lies. "I have what you might say is a knack for finding folks that don't care to be found."

"Well, you have your work cut out, Deputy. I asked all over the county and no one knows where the Cades took off for. Not that anyone knew much of them when they were here. Kept to themselves more than's usual."

Lew imagined there was more than polite inquiries made. If anyone knew anything, they'd have shared it with this scary little sumbitch.

"And you've every reason to want to see them brought to justice, Mr. Taggart."

"Cades killed my boy. Fuck justice. I want them dead. You as good at findin' folks as you say?"

"I have earned a reputation."

"And, what, you arrest their asses and extradite them back to Alabama for trial?"

"That's the job."

"Be easier to leave them where you find them."

"Not sure I take your meaning, sir." Lew damned sure knew what Taggart was getting at.

"It'd be worth ten thousand to know Levon was dead. Another five for his uncle."

Fifteen thousand dollars on top of getting out from under the little gook's thumb.

"Well, given what I know of those old boys, they're sure to resist arrest." Lew let a shadow of a leer cross his face.

"You come on back here with good news and we'll

settle up cash."

"I think I can do what you're asking, sir."

"I ain't askin' nothin'," Rolly said, features darkening, and eyes gone mean. "I ain't offerin' nothin'. I'm not tellin' you anythin'. I'm only sayin' I'd be happy enough to pay the man who told me somethin' I want to hear."

"Yes, sir," Lew nodded eyes lowered.

"Don't never think of fuckin' me, Deputy. We're just two guys talkin' here. I know my rights."

"Yes, sir." Lew set his glass down and stood to go.

"You got any kind of leads or clues or like that?" Rolly said, not standing to see his guest from the porch.

"I have a few lines in the water." Lew made his way down the steps past the big bastard gripping the mongrel's collar to hold it close. Both man and dog offered baleful stares. "Next time you see me I'll have a story you'll want to hear."

"And proof you done what you say you done," Rolly called from the shade of the porch.

Lew waved a hand as he reached the Tundra and slid inside. His shirt was sopping and sticking to his back and gut. Salt sweat stung his eyes where it ran down his brow. The AC came roaring from the vents as he turned the key. The chill he felt was not only from evaporating perspiration.

He made a bootleg turn in the yard to head back along the washboard track. The dogs, led by the mongrel, chased him halfway back to the county road. They only stopped when he jackrabbited the engine to send a spray of red mud over them from the spinning rear wheels.

As he drove back toward Haley and his motel

room and the long shower he'd take, he thought about the man he was set on finding. This Cade fella collected enemies the way Mama Dollinger used to collect jelly jars. And most of them were willing to part with ready cash to have Cade found. More than getting out of this fix with a whole skin, Lew might just wind up with a fat roll to finance a new life somewhere far from here.

But first he needed to go see a lady about some horses.

17

It had been a long, hot ride in the late summer heat.

Back at the barn, Ray ran water over Flame to cool him down before releasing him out to the paddock. He doused the horse's legs first before moving up to the trunk. Flame's flesh rippled under the water. The wash, mixed with sweat, ran cream-colored down the animal's flanks to run into a drain set in the floor. Ray moved wet hands down the animal's snout and up into its mane. Flame playfully nibbled the shoulder of his shirt, nipping at the cloth with big horse lips.

The girls came into the barn while he was putting the hose back up on its rack. They were dressed for riding in jeans and boots. The terrier trotted in behind them to leap up and flop down atop a hay bale.

"You wanna go riding with us, Ray?" Hope asked.

"I just got back from a ride. You father's gonna want to see me," Ray said as he undid Flame's bridle from the tie lines.

Merry followed him as he led the horse to the rear

doors of the barn that led to the fenced paddock.

"What do you think of the place? Will we be able to raise cattle?" she asked as they watched Flame break into a run that stopped short of the other horses grazing in the shade of some dogwoods.

"You could raise a few here. A dozen maybe. You're grass rich but water poor."

"No way to change that?"

"Not without a lot of expense. Too much money to spend on a hobby farm." Ray regretted it as he said it. The girl's narrowed eyes told him he'd stepped over a line.

"You know, I know you don't have a girlfriend in Carey," she said.

"Yeah?" He drew the sliding door closed, the wheels squeaking in the steel track above.

"You're not a very good liar. Did my father or my grandpa tell you to make that up?"

"It was Mr. Ruskin."

"Wes? Who's he trying to protect?" She was smiling.

"I think *me*," Ray grinned, eyes lowered. "From your dad. He doesn't strike me as a man I'd want to be on the bad side of."

"You have no idea." She followed him as he hefted his saddle and blanket up atop a stable wall. The younger girl was pulling the gear they'd need for their ride from the tack room.

"You need help rounding up your rides?" he said.

"We do all right on our own," Merry said, not making a move to help her sister.

"You girls enjoy your reading?" he asked, more to break the silence than out of any interest.

"It wasn't fun reading," Merry shrugged.

"Why not?"

"Nina was reading eighth grade biology. I was reading the teacher's guide for it."

"Don't you have any fun books?"

"Sure. Only this is for homeschooling. I have to read ahead of Nina to stay in front of what she's learning."

"You homeschool her. Who homeschools you?"

"I'm self-teaching. My dad looks over my work. I might take my GED in the spring."

"You going to college after that?"

"Naw," Merry shook her head. "I'm thinking of enlisting in the Marine Corps. Maybe go to school after that."

Ray studied her face for any trace that she was teasing him.

"Come on, Jodie," Hope said from the partly opened door to the paddock. She had bridles and lead lines over her shoulder. "I think Ray has work to do."

"Don't be scared of my dad," Merry said as she moved to join her sister in the sunshine. "I think he likes you."

He looked back as he walked to the house. The girls were approaching the horses, clucking and chucking, offering handfuls of sweet feed. The animals approached at a walk, ears forward. He stopped to watch the girls cut their mounts from the group and bridle them with ease before leading them to the barn for saddling. They did do all right on their own.

Girls and horses, he thought to himself.

"Looks like you made a friend."

Ray turned to see Levon approaching from the

house. The front of his shirt and jeans were gray with dust. He'd been laying block for the addition off the back of the house.

"I was just coming to see you," Ray said. The sound of the girls laughing came from the paddock.

"He doesn't take to everyone." Levon nodded to the Jack Russell standing by Ray and looking up, tail wiggling. Ray hadn't been aware the dog had followed him from the barn.

"A blessing and a curse. Most animals like me."

"I'd figure it would be a job requirement in your line of work. There's still fixin's laid out from lunch. Come get yourself a sandwich and tell me what you saw out there."

Ray nodded and followed Levon back to the house.

18

There was a strange truck, a dusty Toyota, pulled up alongside Sandy's Kia.

Jessie Hamer brought her van to a stop before the barn. She killed the engine and stepped out. The van's headlights remained on, capturing the strange truck in a spotlight. It had been a long day and evening birthing a breeched foal. All she wanted was a cold beer, a hot bath and a plate of warmed up Chinese. She had not the time nor patience for whatever the guy climbing out of the Tundra was selling.

The guy approached over the gravel, wrinkled sport jacket, cowboy boots and shit-eating grin framed by a flame-colored beard. The palest white man Jessie had ever seen, whisps of cornsilk hair standing up in the evening breeze.

"Been waitin' a while," he said as he neared. "Your daughter mighta mentioned me."

"The insurance man? Look, I've had—"

"I'm afraid I'm guilty of a lie. A little white one." The near-albino held up a badge and ID in a leather folder. His smile finally reached his piggy eyes.

She allowed him into the kitchen where he took a seat. Jessie leaned against a counter, not offering him a drink of any kind.

"That little girl of yours told me you were gifted some horses recently."

Jessie fought down the urge to look away.

"One of your neighbors. A man named Cade."

"Not really a neighbor. He's a good ten miles from here."

"Not as the crow flies. Or the horse trots." The pale man licked his lips. "His place is just over that hill out back. Maybe three miles or less."

"You're looking for him and you think I know where he is."

"There was something between you, missy. Something more than being neighborly." The pale man showed teeth.

"Not anymore. He's gone. Out of my life and good riddance."

"Nobody cuts all ties. Nobody just up and runs without some sign of where they're headed. Could be anything from what kind of clothes they packed to a place they might have mentioned in the past."

"I told you---"

"Bullshit, woman," the pale man said, slamming his palm on the tabletop.

"Do you have a warrant?" Jessie said, pushing off the counter.

"I don't need one." The pale man looked hard at her with eyes blue as crystal. "I want your phone now. Your daughter's too. And I find any contact from any Cades on either of them and you both go down for accessory to murder. Homicide one. Your girl's eighteen. You might be on the same block down at Wetumpka. You can try and keep the dykes offa her."

"I'm not showing you anything," Jessie was leaning on the table now. "You come back with some paper and a cop who doesn't talk like bar trash, and I'll cooperate."

The pale man pushed back his chair to stand but clearly had no intention of leaving. A two-tone bell by the kitchen door interrupted whatever he was going to say next.

"What's that?" he asked.

"Entry alarm at the end of the drive," Jessie said. "Someone ran over the hose."

The pale man parted the curtains above the sink to see a vehicle approaching up the drive.

A forest green Range Rover.

"You're gonna wish you talked to me," the pale man said.

19

"I got alla this well in hand," Lew Dollinger said, arms spread as he crossed the yard to the Range Rover.

The big bastard from before was climbing from the driver's side and Roland Taggart from the opposite door. An even bigger bastard, thicker around the middle but a clone of the first one in every other way, untucked himself from the back seat. Must be a formal occasion, Lew thought, they both put on shirts.

"We'll talk inside," Rolly said, making for the door with his sons in tow.

Lew shrugged and followed. He found the new arrivals confronted by the Hamer woman who was doing her best to cover her fear with anger.

"I want you all out of my house right this minute," she said, stabbing a finger at the door.

"I told you, Mr. Taggart. I was handling this," Lew said.

"Junior," Rolly said. "Dex."

Before he could turn, Lew's arms were pinned to his sides by the larger of the two monsters. He was held in a sweaty bear hug that had his boot heels squeaking on the linoleum. Either Junior or Dex had his Glock out of his waistband to tuck into their own.

"You're asking for trouble here, son," Lew said.

"You ain't no deputy," either Junior or Dex said before delivering a rabbit-punch to Lew's gut that sank to the wrist.

"You think I don't have friends down the courthouse, Dollinger?" Rolly said, leaning to place his nose inches from Lew's. Lew fought down the urge to vomit, the other man's face swimming in his vision.

Lew tried to gasp out further dire warnings but all he could do was suck wind.

"Now, you tell me what you told him," Rolly said, turning to the horse doctor standing backed against the refrigerator. She recoiled from him, the back of her blouse brushing some magnets from the front of the Amana. Postcards, mostly featuring horses, fluttered to the floor.

"I didn't tell him anything. There's nothing to tell."

"I asked around about you," Rolly said, leaning with a hand splayed on the refrigerator door. "You and Cade was a hot item till he run off. I figure he must have left you somethin'. A love letter with a forwardin' address maybe?"

"You heard wrong," the woman said, turning away.

"She said she's got nothing," Lew said, voice raw from swallowing a mouthful of bile.

"Shut his mouth," Rolly said.

Lew'd been beat before by experts. These boys

weren't professionals but they'd do till one came along. They lacked the follow through of a true beatdown master but made up for it with enthusiasm. With the fat bastard holding him, Lew couldn't do much to roll with the strikes. Junior or Dex caught him a few solid rights to the cheek and jaw before slamming a fist down on the top of Lew's scalp.

"Shit the bed!" the Taggart sibling yelled, shaking his hand with a pained expression. The punch to the pale man's skull had dislocated two fingers.

The fatter one took over, kneeing Lew in the small of the back before dropping him to the tiles. Then boots went to work on him as he tried to crawl from under the rain of heels and toes. His sight was going gray around the edges when they let up. A booted foot between his shoulders pressed down to keep him in place. He lay there, listening to the conversation through the buzzing in his ears.

"You got a little girl," Rolly's voice came from the other side of kitchen table. "She home?"

The woman's answer was muffled. Or maybe Lew was passing out.

"Go find her," Rolly barked.

The foot came off Lew's back.

"What do we do with the fake lawman, Dad?" said one of the big bastards.

"Toss him in that closet till I'm done here."

Lew felt rough hands under his armpits as he was hauled through the door of a walk-in pantry. They dumped him between shelves of canned goods and jars and slammed the door shut. He heard the click of a lock. Boot soles scuffed the tiles outside and moved away into the house, male voices calling in a sing-song voice.

The tight confines swam around him at cyclone speed as he tried to push off the floor. He squeezed his eyes shut and opened them to find that he'd achieved a sitting position. He could see the light from the kitchen under the crack of the door and scooted on his ass closer to listen.

The Hamer woman was protesting, pleading.

"It's up to you. You tell me where Cade is, and the boys will leave your girl be."

More wordless sounds of pleading.

Teeth gritted, Lew hauled his way up to one knee as he drew the buck knife from the scabbard in his boot.

"Longer you wait the harder it'll be on that little girl."

Lew worked the tip of the knife into the jamb while holding the knob tight in his fist.

"Wait long enough and you won't be sure which one to name the baby after."

Lew, shoulder pressed to the door, listened hard to the woman's whispered response.

"There's a letter. On the door here."

Lew used the knife as a pry to pop the bolt free from the jamb as he shoved the door open.

Rolly Taggart was turning from where he'd plucked an envelope from under a magnet on the refrigerator door. His eyes went wide as Lew, bloody, deranged and near white as a snowman, closed on him.

The buck knife came up in an underhanded arc to catch the shorter man just back of the chin. Lew closed with him to grip the back of Taggart's skull to drive the curved tip of the blade upward. Through the palm of his hand, Lew felt the wet impact of the knife piercing first the soft palate and then scraping bone on its way to the base of the brain.

Taggart fell from his grasp, lifeless and with remarkably little blood spilled.

Lew stooped, chest heaving, to retrieve the dropped envelope from the floor. With his other hand he unbuckled the boot holster that held his hammerless Smith. The horse doctor stepped away, eyes staring and mouth slack. With a groan, Lew straightened up once again, his lower back and sides aflame. He'd for damned sure be pissing blood come morning.

He pocketed the envelope and backed away. One hand on the wall for support, Lew following the sounds from deeper in the house. The low voices of the brothers interspersed with some kind of animal bleats. A door at the end of the hall stood partly opened. It was decorated with colorful stickers of flowers and cartoon ponies.

Junior and Dex had the girl he talked to the other day on a white canopy bed, bare-ass, belly down and legs spread. The fatter one held her by the wrists, arms taut. The other was struggling to undo his belt.

Lew put two in the chest of fatty. The big man fell forward with a childish pout to crush the squirming girl to the mattress.

The other turned stumbling with his cut-offs around his ankles and dick swinging free. Lew put a .38 through his skull that starred a vanity mirror behind him. The man, Junior or Dex, stumbled back with a howl like a lost dog. A second round turned the shriek to a gurgle as it tore out his throat. He dropped kicking and gagging to the floor. Lew stepped closer to put the last round in the hammerless into the man's brain. The man lay still on the carpet.

Lew crouched with a wince to take back his Glock. He rounded the bed and hauled the fat man off the girl. She clambered backwards over the bed, pulling bloody bed covers with her. Using the Glock, Lew pumped two more rounds into the tub of lard lying by the bed.

"You're all right, honey," he said, voice flat. "Run on to your mama."

A sheet wrapped about her, the girl disappeared from the room. Lew followed.

He found the two of them in the kitchen, the woman calming her daughter, holding her close. The girl shivered, the shock wearing off.

"She'll have some bad dreams is all," Lew said by way of reassurance. "They hadn't got down to business."

"What do we do now?" the woman said.

"Well, you two think up the story of how this all happened." Lew was at the sink rubbing down the Glock and Smith with a dry dishrag. He dropped them on the drainboard next to some dinner dishes.

"We need to call the police," she said.

"Indeed, you do." Lew ran the dishrag over the area of the tabletop where he'd been sitting as well as the chair back. "Only I think we'd both agree that you owe me the courtesy of at least an hour's head start."

"What do I tell them?" Jessie asked.

"I'd suggest a home invasion," Lew said, nodding sagely as he crouched to remove a fat wad of bills from the late Rolly Taggart's pants pocket. He slid the ring with the fat stone off the dead man's pinky and onto his own. "You're a vet, right? Got all kinds of drugs somewhere a junkie'd be after. Things went wild west and you and the girl came out on top."

"They'll believe that?"

"Trust me, doc. They'll *want* to believe it and that's all that'll matter." He stuffed the wad of cash in a pocket next to the envelope. "Alla these fellas have long criminal records."

"And the guns?"

"Not registered. You can say you bought them from Mr. Cade for home protection. They'll confiscate them. I'd suggest you head over to Rural King in the morning and pick yourself up a shotgun. Two women living alone? Only makes sense."

"I suppose I should thank you," she said as he stepped to the door, the girl's face buried in her shoulder.

"No need, ma'am," he said, patting the pocket that contained he envelope. "I got what I came for."

20

"The horses are gone!" Hope said as she burst into the kitchen from the front room.

Fern was scrambling eggs while Levon and Wesley sat at the table drinking their first coffees of the day. The dogs were waiting patiently, snouts in the air to take in the scent of frying bacon.

"Which horses?" Levon said, standing.

"*All* of them!" Merry said, coming in on her sister's heels.

The dogs were stirred up now. Rascal yipping and leaping up to place forepaws on Merry's shins. The hound looking on with doleful eyes.

"Slow down, honey," Levon said. Merry's eyes were streaming, her mouth twisted to fight back tears.

"We went to let them out and the stalls are empty! They are gone!" Hope said, tugging on Levon's shirt sleeve.

"Go get Ray," Levon said to Wesley who had already pushed away from the table to rise. "Meet me at the barn."

The stalls were open as well as the rear door that led to the paddock. The Jack Russell bolted through and out into the field yapping as he ran. The bluetick loped after him. Levon followed the dogs to find them gathered at a black and white shape lying in the grass fifty yards in back of the barn. It was the goat, Tricky Dick. He lay with dead eyes staring in a black pool of blood alive with flies.

"Throat's cut," Levon said to Merry who'd joined him. "By someone who has experience."

"Why kill Junebug?" she said, the original name for the pet goat before Fern re-dubbed it for the former president.

"To stop him making noise. Waking up the dogs."

"That means someone *took* them."

"Looks that way," Levon headed for what looked like a gap in the back fence.

Ray came up at a run as Levon and Merry reached a place where the rails had been removed from the posts. The grass had been trampled flat by the passage of hooves.

"Any signs of a vehicle?" Ray said as he slowed to join them.

"No. They got them out of the barn and herded them this way." Levon pointed north. "The dogs would have heard a truck come this close."

"They won't be hard to follow," Ray said. "A blind man could read that sign. And, anyway, they'll be heading for the fire road. They'll have a trailer up there."

"You think so?" Levon said. "You've seen this road?"

"Yes, sir. Only thing that makes sense. Saw fresh dirt bike tracks when I was up there. Should've mentioned it."

"Could just be kids." Levon was heading back across the paddock toward the buildings. Ray alongside, Merry trotting to keep up.

"What'll we do?" Merry asked. The dogs joined them as they neared the barn.

"Call state police maybe," Ray said.

"No. There's maybe four state cops covering six counties," Levon said. "They'd be most of the day getting here if they came at all."

"We got no horses to follow them," Ray said.

"We'll take the pickup. It'll manage this ground just fine."

"You mean, you and me? A posse?" Ray said.

"Get what you need and meet me at the truck," Levon said.

"I'm going with you," Merry said as Ray ran to his trailer.

"You're not," Levon said climbing behind the wheel of the Ford. "I need you to ride to the Bingham's five miles west on the county road. They need to know what happened. Take the El Camino. Wes will take the 4Runner to the Tollhouse Ranch and tell them. Both of you take radios along."

Ray had come up, his Henry rifle in a cloth case under his arm.

"You think you'll need that?" Levon said.

"Better to have it and not need it than need it and not have it," Ray said and slid the rifle onto the back seat along with a box of shells. "You have something? Maybe a pistol?"

"I'll be fine," Levon said, gunning the truck to life once Ray was in the cab. "Remember, honey. Head to Bingham's and tell them our stock's been stolen.

Tell Wes to go to the Tollhouse place."

"I will," Merry said stepping back.

"And your sister is to stay here with Fern," Levon called as he spun the truck out of the space and aimed it for the rear property line and north.

"You call your father 'Fern'?" Ray asked, hanging on the hand strap as the truck trundled over the rough ground.

"It's a term of affection," Levon said, eyes ahead. "But don't tell him I called him that."

Levon turned the truck to follow the swath of crushed grass flattened by the passage of the five horses. They reached the place where the trail crossed the fire road. The hoof prints showed that the animals had been led directly across the road and into the grasslands to the north. Both men got out of the truck to inspect the ground.

"There goes my theory shot in the ass," Ray said, dropping to a knee to look at the soft ground along the verge of the road.

"What can you see?" Levon asked.

"I only see tracks for our five. There's no new tracks for bikes or an ATV. That means whoever took them came on foot and rode off on our mounts."

"How many do you figure?"

At least three," Ray brushed at some of the tracks with a sheaf of grass he'd broken off. "From the impressions I think three of our horses have riders on them."

"When did they pass here?"

"Hard to say. It was before it got light. It's only a guess but I think they have at least two hours on us."

"Where are they headed?"

"North, sir. They're looking to put distance

between them and the ranch. What's up that way?"

"Miles and miles of nothing."

"Is there maybe another fire road farther north?" Ray said, squinting into the distance.

"I don't know. Maybe. It's all open range clear to the mountains." Levon regarded the blue blur between the land and the sky that defined the horizon.

"Maybe they were eco-nuts. You know, animal rights types, letting horses go free."

"No. They killed the goat. This is something else. Let's head back." Levon turned to the truck.

"You change your mind about the cops?" Ray said.

"No. We need the horse trailer and we need a map."

"For what?"

"We're going after them on horseback," Levon said, turning the truck around on the fire road in a thick cloud of yellow dust. "It's either that or face two brokenhearted little girls and know I didn't do anything about it."

"A real no-bullshit posse," Ray said and swallowed hard to keep the excitement from his voice.

21

"All our stock's still here where they should be," Kathryn Bingham told the young girl who'd arrived in a hurry in the stable yard.

Merry stood in a three-sided courtyard formed by a hay barn, machine building and stable with a couple dozen stalls. Some workers in coveralls were mucking stalls, pushing loaded barrows to a steaming mountain of manure piled in a roofless block-walled enclosure. A pair of men, who looked like working cowboys, were saddling mounts. Another was gassing up an ATV. She turned back to the woman, an attractive lady with silver gray hair tied back.

"You're sure?" Merry asked.

"My husband's already back from riding the line," Kathryn said. "No breaks. And we don't let our horses out to graze until we know there's no breaks. How many did you lose?"

"Five. All quarter horses," Merry said. "They just came and took them sometime early this morning, we think. Right out of their stalls."

"There was some of that up in Shoshone County but that was a couple of years back."

"What happened to those horses?"

"Slaughter yards," Kathryn winced in apology. "There's a yard over outside Bogel Station. They mostly transship to packers up in Alberta."

"What's the name of the place in Bogel Station?" Merry had a rough idea of where that town was.

"I'll ask my husband." Kathryn took a satellite phone off her belt and tabbed in a number.

While Mrs. Bingham spoke to her husband, Merry looked about the stable yard and the fenced grassland that rolled down toward the county road. The green fields were dotted with black angus cows. She lost count at fifty-two before Kathryn got off the phone.

"It's an outfit called Bel-Mar. They have stockyards down near the freight station. Mr. Bingham says it's a French company owns it though they do a lot of shipping to Japan."

"Who'd want to eat a horse?"

"Don't ask me, honey. Not when there's plenty of good beef in the world."

"Maybe my dad and I'll head over there," Merry said, turning back to the El Camino. "Thank you for your help."

"Thanks for the heads-up," Kathryn said with a wave. "And good luck."

Merry drove back toward the road along the drive lined either side by steel cattle fencing. A few of the big animals poked their heads through the poles to pluck at weeds growing along the lip of a drainage ditch.

The woman at the ranch had not offered any real

comfort but still Merry felt a bit calmer. Maybe it was just having some of her questions answered. None of this made any sense to her. She thought, far as they lived from any kind of town or highway, that there'd be no one out here to harm them or steal from them. No place was safe. She felt naïve, even childish, to have let herself feel so easy in their new home. She'd felt safe back at Uncle Fern's place in Alabama and look how that turned out. They were on the run again, living under made-up names. She wondered if someday they'd have hidden in every corner of the country until they ran out of places to run to.

Two miles down the long drive, she turned the El Camino left onto the county road and pointed it toward home. She was anxious to get back and find out what her father might have learned about whoever stole their horses. Halfway back along the county road she could see a vehicle approaching from the east. It wasn't until it had barreled past her that she realized it was her daddy's pickup hauling their horse trailer.

She stood on the brakes to whip the wheel around in a sloppy bootleg turn that took her off the highway in a wide arc. Spraying clods of earth, she powered back the way she came to follow the Ford until it made the turn into Bingham's.

***

"My advice to you is to let the law handle this," Jack Bingham said as he took a seat hipshot on the edge of a picnic table in the shade of a canvas tent set up over an outdoor barbecue area.

"Those horses will be long gone before I can get

any answers," Levon said. "And we know which way they went."

"They could be in Montana by the time you caught up with them," Jack said, nodding away to the northeast.

Merry joined them, running from the El Camino pulled up to the Bingham house now. It was a sprawling stone rancher with low steel roofs nestled in some old oaks and rangy firs. Kathryn Bingham had come out with a tray of coffee and biscuits.

"Or they could be taking their time thinking no one's after them," Levon said. "You're the nearest place with horses. I'd like to buy two. Price is no object."

"You'll need at least four if you're serious about catching these fellas up," Kathryn suggested.

"She's right, sir," Ray added. "We'd need to spell the mounts if we're gonna be covering any distance by dark."

"Well, I won't sell you any of my stock," Jack said. "But if your mind is set on going after them, I'll loan you four mounts. Worse comes to worse, and you don't recover your animals, we can discuss a price for buying replacements."

"That's very generous," Levon said, extending a hand which Mr. Bingham took in his.

"Maybe. Mostly, I'm willing to buck the odds that you'll find these bastards. That's in my interest. I could even lend you a couple of my hands to go with you. I'd go with you myself if I thought I wouldn't slow you down."

"Thank you. But I think it's better it's just Ray and me traveling light."

"What about me?" Merry asked.

"I need you to be looking after things back home," Levon said.

"Don't patronize me, Daddy," she said, eyes narrowed.

"Your sister's gonna need you close," he said. "You know how she feels about Felicia. She'll need her big sister."

Merry nodded and turned to the El Camino to head home.

Levon walked a path to the stables with Jack and Kathryn Bingham while Ray drove the truck and trailer down toward the stable yard.

"I guess this is what I should have expected from folks of frontier stock," Levon said.

Mrs. Bingham laughed.

"Frontier stock! Jack owned a Nissan dealership in Santa Monica before we moved here!"

22

Lew Dollinger drove all night after leaving the animal doctor heading roughly west on county and state roads to avoid any traffic cams.

The night sky was turning from black to slate when he pulled into a truck stop in Holy Springs, Mississippi for coffee and an egg sandwich. He sat in a booth and remembered the envelope he'd taken from Roland Taggart's corpse. After gulping down a handful of Advils, he fished the envelope out from where it lay folded beside the wad of cash in his coat pocket. He'd count that later. He flattened the envelope out on the greasy countertop before lifting it to his eyes to read the neatly written out address. 'Jessie Hamer' was written in careful script above 'Riverstone Veterinary and the address. No return address.

He drew the envelope closer and closed one eye to focus. The postmark was a bit blurred but readable.

Carey, Idaho.

He undid the flap and pulled out a single sheet of paper folded three times. There was a message on the otherwise-unmarked sheet in the same hand that addressed the envelope.

> *Jessie,*
> *This is for keeping Montana, Penny and Bravo. Montana likes fuji apples if you could buy him some.*
> *All our love to you and Sandy.*
> *M & H*

Merry and Hope. The Cade daughters.

Where the hell was Carey, Idaho? It couldn't be a big town or he'd have heard of it. And, from what he could recall from school, Idaho was a big-ass state. The only other thing he knew about it was they grew potatoes.

Next Walmart he passed he'd need to pick up a fresh burner and see what he could learn about Carey. And, somewhere, he'd need to buy another gun to replace the two he left behind in Alabama. Something unregistered. That meant expensive unless he got creative.

Later in the morning, the sun full up, Lew pulled up to the pump island at a mom-and-pop outside Memphis. He stayed away from the chain stations even though it meant paying more per gallon. Too many cameras at the chain places. Too many ways to track a man in this new age.

Paid in cash too. That black card sitting in his wallet was a leash. First time he used it the tidy little gook he met back in Punta Gordo would be on him like his Aunt Marie at the Golden Corral cake trays.

He was aware of the days he was using up. It meant he was half on the hunt and half on the run. Should his trip west come up a dry hole, he'd just keep on driving. Put distance and time between himself and the little gook and whoever he worked for. Fail to find Levon Cade and they'd come looking for him. Best he could do was outrun them as long as possible.

Inside the cramped little food mart, he paid a fat colored gal for fifty bucks in unleaded and a coffee and some Slim Jims. Place smelled like bacon and sour milk. Outside, he flipped open the little door on the Tundra to access the fuel intake. Something was jamming the gas cap as he tried to loosen it. He plucked out a little teardrop of blue plastic with a keychain loop on it.

"Ever seen one of these?" he said to a colored kid pumping gas into a Nissan on the other side of the pump island.

"Sure. That's an RFID," the kid said.

"And what the fuck's an ar-eff-eye-dee?" Goddamn kid showing off.

"It's a radio frequency ID. People hook 'em to stuff they lose alla the time. Car keys. Wallets. Tried to get my mama to put one on the TV remote she's always losin'."

"It's a transmitter?"

"Yeah. Sends out a signal."

"What's the range?"

"I dunno. Couple miles?"

Lew regarded the sky-blue plastic chip in his fingers. Unlikely the gook planted it there. He'd gassed up a couple times since Punto Gordo. He'd have noticed it. And they'd have to practically be driving up his ass all this time to stay in range.

More likely the Taggarts put it there while he was at their place. The Tundra was out of his sight when he was up on their porch. Explained how they found him at the animal doctor's.

Or the very real possibility that the tidy little man had his two enforcers tracking Lew this minute. They could be somewhere out of sight right now waiting for him to move on.

He turned to toss it in a trash bin that was set between the pumps. Lew hesitated, the key ring around the end of his finger. The kid was replacing the pump handle on the opposite pump.

"Hey, kid. Where you headed?" Lew asked, leaning between the pumps.

"Back to school. Wake Forest."

"That's back east? North Carolina?"

"Winston-Salem. Yeah."

"Tell you what, you take this along with you a ways," Lew said, dangling the blue chip between his fingers. "When you get round about Atlanta, you toss it out the window."

"What for?" The kid tilted his head with a wary look.

"I want to fuck with my ex-wife. Must be her put this on me. Her and the dumb sumbitch she took up with."

"How much?" The kid tilted his head the other way.

"A twenty?"

"Forty."

They closed the deal and the kid drove off the lot with the cash and the transponder. Seemed cheap enough for a little peace of mind. Lew fueled up the Tundra and decided he'd pull over once he reached Arkansas and give the truck a thorough going-over for any other bugs, radio senders or what-the-hell might be planted inside.

23

The Ram sat up on the fire road with the horse trailer hitched behind with ramp down. Wes held the reins of the two saddled horses and watched while Levon and Ray tied down saddle packs on the other two. The borrowed mounts were all geldings, a gray, two chestnuts and blue roan. Sleeping bags, coats, a change of socks, some gallon water jugs, a small camp stove and food for two days.

"That's the wrong hat if you're gonna play cowboy," Wes said.

"Ray's the only cowboy here," Levon said and tugged a Skoal Bandit ball cap onto his head.

"You might want to re-think taking a weapon along," Ray said as he secured his Henry in a leather scabbard secured to his saddle. "These guys aren't gonna give up your horses easy."

"I told you I had that covered." Levon pulled the rear door of the Ram's crew cab open and dropped the rear seatback. There were two shotguns and a rifle hung on the back wall of the cab. Levon pulled out a modified M4. He slid it into a ripstop case and filled the four magazine pouches.

"Shit," Ray said. "We going to war?"

"What did you say about needing but not having?"

Levon slung the strap of the rifle case from the saddle horn of the roan so it was pointed barrel down and easily accessible.

"You got your prick with you?" Wes said as he handed the lead lines of the pack horses off.

Ray was confused until Levon touched the walkie talkie that dangled from his belt with a nod. They called radios pricks. He knew Wesley and his boss were former military though they hardly ever talked about it. It was more in the way they handled themselves. Here they were, him and Mr. Holman, setting off to hunt down men, and the boss treated it like just another Tuesday. The assured way Mr. Holman handled that rifle of his said a lot about the man. He'd been shot at in anger and shot back the same spirit somewhere in his past. And something told Ray it was way more than a time or two.

"Give a holler if you need anything," Wes said, stepping back as they reined the horses around.

"Like what?" Levon said as he followed Ray north of the fire road.

"An airstrike?"

"Just do what you can to keep the girls' minds off the horses."

"I'll run over to Jerome and pick up pizzas tonight. We'll have a movie night."

And nothing with horses in it, Wes thought as he watched the men and animals head up a gradual slope and over a ridgeline. He waited until they were out of sight before getting in the Ram to head back down the fire road to the county two-lane that would take him to Elysium.

***

"Any idea who we might be trailing?" Levon said drawing even with Ray as they followed the trail of hoofprints and parted grass across a broad level plain.

"I guess we'd call them rustlers," Ray said. "They'll be looking to sell them for meat. Not much of a reason other than that for stealing stock."

"There's no controls on selling horse flesh? No restrictions?"

"It's like anything else. Where there's money, the rules can be bent. Brands, papers, stuff like that won't matter to some buyers."

"What kind of money we talking here? They make dogfood out of horses, right?"

"That's been illegal for a long time in the USA. No ponies in your Alpo since way before I was born. It's good money now. Horse meat goes for about the same price as veal in Europe or Japan."

"The Binghams told me the Japanese ship them live," Levon said.

"Yeah. Koreans and Indonesians too. But those companies are strictly by the book. More than likely these guys are trading off the books with packers shipping frozen carcasses or canned meat to France or Germany or other places like that," Ray said.

"Meat is meat to them, I guess."

"Doesn't make it right, sir. Horses and men have a

special bond. Dogs too. Goes back a long way, right? I'm no animal rights nut. I like a good ham or roast. But eating this animal here would be like eating a friend."

"Like a pet."

"Horses aren't pets. Not working horses. Working dogs neither. There's a bond there deeper than a show pony or a lap dog."

"You're a bit of philosopher, Ray."

"Show me someone who works stock that isn't."

***

By afternoon they'd come to broken country. Gullies and trenches that came down from higher ground to join the dry wash. There'd be water here in the spring. Snow melt. The trail was harder to pick out in places across the rock scatter. They were forced to ride a serpentine pattern now and then to pick it up again.

Their mounts were tiring so they stopped to switch the saddles to the re-mounts and the packs to the roan and gray.

Ray had time to assess his boss' riding skills. The man sat well, and his handling was proficient. He knew the gear too and did a good job bridling and cinching. In general, he seemed to understand horses and was easy atop one. He'd told Ray that he didn't ride for fun, but the man *could* ride. It was a sure sign that Mr. Holman had spent a lot of time in the saddle at one time. It only served to deepen the mystery surrounding the man he worked for. He wished he'd been able to ask his Uncle Jimmy about his new employer. But, from what little he saw, he decided he liked Mr. Holman. It helped that his boss had respect for his skills and left him in charge of this hunt even though Mr. Holman obviously had some experience tracking men.

"See that cleft ahead?" Ray said, standing in the stirrups of a chestnut and pointing a rein end.

"I see it." Levon finished drawing the buckles of his bridle in place and looked north to see an interruption in the chain of hills ahead of them. There was a gap between two sugar loaf rises, the gray walls of the mountains rising beyond.

"That looks to me where they're heading," Ray said, retaking his seat. "Don't know where these guys are taking your horses. Map says there's nothing up there but peaks and valleys. Nothing like a town or even a state road all the way to the Montana border."

"What kind of time are they making?"

"We're gaining on them is my guess. They have no idea anyone's on their back trail. But they've still got a half day's lead or more."

"And we're only a few hours from sunset. Think they'll camp?"

"I don't know. But we'll have to. Maybe at the mouth of that pass there'll be a good spot with shelter in the rocks."

"Up to you," Levon said, swinging up in the saddle.

An hour's ride brought them closer to the pass between the two hills. That's where they saw the first buzzards.

24

With the horses gone and the stalls still clean from that morning, Merry and Hope found their daily routine disrupted. They sat in the shade of the veranda, books open and unread on their laps.

"I made some grilled cheese sandwiches the way you like," Fern said, leaning from the open screen door. Rascal prodded past to join the girls, nails clicking on the flags.

"We're not that hungry," Merry said. The dog put his forepaws on the arm of the porch chair, stubby tail wiggling.

"Sliced the tomatoes real thin. Slivered onions too," Fern said, forcing a cheery note into his voice.

"Maybe later." Merry pulled the insistent dog up into her lap by the collar.

"They'll get greasy sitting out."

Both girls fixed Fern with a stare that sent him retreating back into the house.

"What can we do?" Hope said.

"Wait." Merry idly scratched the stiff hair behind Rascal's ears. The dog responded with a blissed-out expression of adoration.

"Will they find the horses?"

"I don't know. They have to catch up with the men who took them."

"Why would men take them?" Hope swung her legs to sit sideways at the end of her chaise.

"The Binghams said that sometimes horses are taken for food. They're stolen and taken to a slaughterhouse."

Hope turned her eyes to the floor.

"I can't imagine anyone eating a horse," Merry said.

"If someone was very hungry, they would."

"This isn't about being hungry. The Binghams said that the horses are shipped all over the world. Horse meat is a delicacy. Rich people eat it."

"All over the world?" Hope said and looked out to the empty paddock. "How will Ray and Daddy find them riding horses?"

"I've been thinking about that. What if Ray and Daddy are wrong? What if Dusty and Felicia—"

"And Charlie."

"—are already on a truck heading for a meat plant? And by the time Daddy gets back it'll be too late."

Merry shifted the terrier off her lap and he leapt to the floor to run in circles as she rose.

"Come on with me, Hopey," she said as she stepped from the porch.

Hope followed her toward the barn.

25

They came on the carcass just as the shadows were filling the pass.

Their arrival caused a blanket of turkey vultures to part, revealing the animal lying dead on the rock scree that covered the sloping ground. Ray pulled his lever action free to fire a round that would scatter the birds. Levon reached out from his saddle to grab the barrel.

"No need for that." Levon dismounted and picked up a rock. He heaved it at a collection of the buzzards, nearly striking one. They leapt skyward to flap away, silent as phantoms, to the ledges above.

They left their mounts ground reined to climb the slope to where what remained of the horse lay.

It was Dusty, Merry's buckskin mare with a sprinkle of cinnamon across its chest and rump.

"Who'd do this to an animal?" Ray said, his throat tight.

The horse lay on its side and there were signs where the birds had been at the soft flesh. The eyes, ears and belly had been pecked and clawed. The signs of men were here too. The rear legs had been cut away at the haunches and sawn off at the hocks. The cannons lay where they'd been tossed, hooves still shod.

It had been quickly done but by an expert hand. Long strips down the flanks had been trimmed down to where ribs gleamed. The snout, from just below the eyes had been cut and peeled from the bone. Yellow teeth in white bone set in a hideous grin. The air at this altitude was cooler than down below or the carcass would already be covered in flies.

"They butchered it for the meat they could carry." Levon crouched down by the quarter horse. "Maybe it went lame, was slowing them down."

"So, they tortured it?" Ray looked away.

"No. They shot it first." Levon pulled the mane aside to reveal two puckered holes just behind the gnawed flesh of what was left of an ear. Keyhole shaped wounds scorched black all around with powder burns. A military weapon fired at close range.

"It doesn't make sense, Mr. Holman."

"What about it doesn't make sense?"

"It looks like these guys know what they're doing. Then butcher it like that? Even the black-market meat houses only buy on the hoof."

"Unless they were going to eat it themselves." Levon said, standing. "Maybe this isn't about selling them on."

"Someone's stealing horses just to eat them? That's Big Foot stuff."

"Then where are they going? You said there's nothing in front of us but more badlands. They could have cut east a few times to find a road, a place where they could have transport waiting."

"Well, stopping to cut up this mare took time, sir. We're getting closer."

"Only we can't follow at night. The ground's rough from here up. Even if it weren't, I wouldn't want to catch up to them in the dark."

"I'd like to catch up to them any time," Ray said between his teeth.

"You think I'm looking forward to telling my little girl her horse is dead?"

"Sorry, sir."

"We're gonna walk our mounts in a wide circle around this until we're up in those trees and then we're gonna make camp. Then we're up before first light and after these motherfuckers."

"Yes, sir."

***

They camped cold, only starting up the camp stove long enough to boil water for coffee after seeing to the horses. It was always the horses first. They unsaddled the chestnuts and unpacked the gray and roan. They hitched them to the boles of some stout firs using the lead lines. They rubbed them down before watering and feeding them

There was a real snap in the air now and they put pull-ons over their work shirts over which they buttoned coats, Levon a flannel-lined barn coat and Ray a fleece hoodie. They ate sandwiches cold in the wavering glow of the stove.

"You think we need to stand a watch?" Ray asked.

"What would a cowboy do?" Levon asked.

"We're way past what a cowboy would do," Ray

said smirking. "At least nowadays since the only savage redskin we have to look out for is me."

"I'll stay up a while. I don't think the men we're after would turn back to check for pursuit. Wouldn't hurt to keep an eye or ear open until it's full dark."

"I'm not sure I can sleep, sir."

"Just get in your bag to keep warm then. We're gonna need the rest for tomorrow."

Ray lay in his bag and pulled the zipper closed, resting his shoulders against the hump of his saddle. His boss turned the dial down on the camp stove. The blue-tinged flicker died to nothing and the shadows between the trees closed in all around. After a few moments, Ray could make out the humped shape of Mr. Holman crouched ten feet away, an indigo shape against the greater black. The man was unmoving, head up and listening. The only sounds were the whisper of the wind dropping down from the mountains to brush the tops of the tall pines. He had every intention of staying awake to keep guard alongside his boss but was soon sound asleep and dreaming of black birds wheeling against a sky yellow as flame.

26

It was bitter cold in the hours before sunrise. The girls could see their breath as they tip-toed through the screen door for the veranda, their boots held in their hands. The flag stones were like ice under their stocking feet. Merry eased the doors closed taking special care to prevent the screen door's hinges from squealing. It wasn't Fern or Wes they worried about waking. It was the dogs. They sat down on the front steps to pull on their boots.

The girls had spent the afternoon and evening of the day before assembling what they would need and stowing it in two backpacks inside the cab of the El Camino. Fern and Wes, unsure of how to deal with two grieving and fretting young ladies, gave them a wide berth. That made it easier for Merry and Hope to make their plans.

The hardest part would be getting the El Camino far enough from the house before starting the engine. The day before, the girls had driven down to the feed store in Jerome with the excuse of getting themselves some ice cream. The men were pleased to see them go, thinking it was just the thing to get their minds off the missing horses for a while.

Merry and Hope did drive to Jerome but only because there was a Wi-Fi hotspot there. Merry was able to look up local slaughterhouses on her smart phone. The nearest, and most likely, was Bel-Mar Processing. It was the one the Binghams mentioned. It was a couple hours north near the Montana border. Merry googled the directions and stored them on her phone.

Once back at Elysium, Merry backed the car up so it sat on a slight grade with its nose pointed down toward the drive. When Wes asked why they hadn't pulled up to the house, Hope told him they planned on giving the car a wash later and wanted to park near the water stand they used to fill buckets for the horses.

They did wash the El Camino later on, smuggling the stuff they'd need for their trip out to the car in water buckets.

Now, Hope was behind the steering wheel and the shifter in neutral. Merry put her shoulder to the tailgate and dug in her heels to give the car a shove. It broke free of the gravel and began to roll down the grade. It picked up speed and Merry climbed onto the back bumper and into the bed. Leaning around the cab, Merry offered Hope hushed directions on steering and warned her not to touch the brake.

After rolling a few minutes the driveway leveled and the car drifted to a stop. Merry climbed down and Hope slid over to allow her behind the wheel. The El Camino gunned to life. A backward glance to see if any lights came on at the house. Merry tapped the gas and they rolled on the county road, turning on the headlights only after they were well into the trees.

***

Hours later, after driving mostly empty roads, they came to Bogel Station.

Google Go directed them to a service road the other side of the flyspeck town that was little more than a gas stop and a trailer park. The road ran alongside train tracks. Merry drove by a long row of livestock cars before arriving at a cyclone fence topped with razor wire.

The Bel-Mar plant sat off to one side of the tracks on several hundred acres of table land. The girls could see low buildings with metal rooftops through the mesh of the fence. There were high wooden fences behind the buildings.

"I don't see any horses," Hope said.

"You can smell them," Merry said, her head out the open driver window.

Hope turned to her with a fragile smile.

They pulled up to an entrance, the first break in the fence line. A block guardhouse sat between the two lanes of a driveway. A faded metal sign on the guardhouse was decorated with the Bel-Mar logo; a silhouette of a horsehead inside the company name in a circle. A rail spur ran in through the entrance back toward the buildings at the rear of the lot. There was a paved parking lot before a steel-sided building with windows across the front.

A guard, wearing a short sleeve shirt with a badge above the breast pocket and a company patch on the shoulder, stepped from the guardhouse and held up a hand for them to stop.

"You girls lost?" the guard said, squinting through tinted glasses.

"We're not lost," Merry said. "This is the place we're looking for."

"We don't sell meat here. This isn't a retail outlet," the guard said by rote as if for the millionth time.

"We're not here to buy meat," Merry said.

"We're looking for our horses!" Hope said, leaning over Merry.

"Well, we don't have them here," the guard said. "If they ran off, this is about the last place they'd come."

"They didn't run off!" Hope announced. "They were stolen!"

"Ain't no stolen horses here," the guard said. "We buy them legal through agents."

"Maybe there was a mistake," Merry said. "Can't we come in and look around?"

"No way in hell that's happening," the guard said with a dry chuckle. "Turn this shit-box around and—"

"Trouble, Stu?" A man in a shiny new pickup had pulled up to the opposite side of the guardhouse on his way out.

"No trouble, Mr. Melnick," the guard said, turning away. "Just some animal nuts is all. Troublemakers."

"That's not true!" Hope said, shouting now. Merry recoiled in surprise. She'd never heard her little sister raise her voice before.

The man in the truck stepped from the cab and crossed the drive to them.

"What's not true?" he said. He looked out of place in a tailored suit worn over a pressed shirt, the collar open. He had a weathered face behind dark glasses.

"We're not activists, sir," Merry said. "We had our horses, five of them, stolen right out of our barn last night."

"Where was this?"

"Our ranch, a couple hours south of here."

"We don't buy stock unless it's from a licensed agent," the man said, insistent but not unkind.

"Couldn't someone maybe have sold stolen stock to one of those agents?" Merry asked. "Maybe without them knowing?"

The man leaned on the sill of the El Camino to consider this. He pushed off and turned to the guard.

"Stu, call Ed Teal. Tell him we have two girls want to take a tour."

27

They were up well before first light to water and feed the horses. Cold sandwiches for themselves before packing and saddling the mounts. Levon and Ray were on the move and heading deeper into the water gap as the first rays of dawn touched the far peaks.

The other side of the cleft opened onto rolling hills of grass that looked to go on to the very foot of the granite range. Tall stalks of mountain brome tossed back and forth as if by invisible currents under the rising sun. The trail of the stolen horses still stood out plain as a swath cut through the waist-high growth. It followed along the edge of a dry wash that ran down the center of the gap.

Three hours' ride brought them to the edge of a broad wadi where snow melt had pooled in the spring. It was a low point surrounded on all sides by banks of sandy mud. A pond of brown water remained at the center. They let the horses water while Ray walked the perimeter.

"They camped here," Ray said, squatting by a place up on the bank where the grass had been crushed flat.

Levon joined him, dropping to a knee. A circle of gray ash banked with earth. The remains of a cook fire made of grass twists. A discarded can of Del Monte corn and another of white beans. The stubs of a few cigarettes, the familiar speckled filters of Marlboros.

"Those prints are from US army issued boots," Levon said, pointing out the deep impressions in the mud. "Looks like your guess of three men was right. I can pick out two different shoe sizes. One of those is worn at the heels and one isn't."

"So, we're outnumbered," Ray said, standing and looking off toward the mountains.

"Only they don't know we're coming," Levon touched the ashes. They were stone cold.

"That how the math works out to you? Surprise gives us a one-man advantage?"

"It's an uncertain science with a lot of variables," Levon admitted.

They walked down the bank to where the horses stood in the shallows, still tanking up.

"And they could be meeting up with more of their friends. They could be loading those horses onto transport right now," Ray said as they walked.

"I don't think that's likely. Does this seem like common stock thievery?"

"No. It does not," Ray said, taking the reins of his chestnut in hand. "They came a long way to get down to your place. It looks like they came on foot. Must have taken them days on foot."

"And they know horses. That suggest anything to you?" Levon led his mount and packy up the bank.

"Indians in army boots? I don't think so, sir."

"At least one weapon too. The gunshot wounds on Dusty looked like mil-spec to me. An AR or something similar."

"ARs are common as dirt out here. Everyone's got at least one," Ray said with a shake of his head.

"The dead horse was hit with a double tap. The close proximity of the wounds looks like an automatic weapon to me."

"Sounds crazy but could they be deserters? Maybe there's an army base up this way."

"There's a Navy Surface Warfare base at Sandpoint," Levon said.

"A Navy base? Idaho is landlocked."

"It's there."

"You been there, sir?"

Levon nodded.

"This is something else," Levon said. "I don't know what it is, but I've got a feeling I don't like."

"Spider-sense tingling?" Ray said with a crooked smile.

Levon gave him a squint.

"Spider-man. From the comic books."

"Hm," Levon said and took the lead to walk his horses onto the trail. "We need to stay off the skyline. I want us to walk awhile. At least till we top this ridgeline."

Ray nodded and followed, urging the chestnut forward with a light tug on the reins. The gray followed on a lead line.

He looked past Levon and up the trail to the path left by the stolen horses and the men who took them. It led up from the waterhole and into the grass once more. The boot prints and the campfire were the first real sign of the men they were after. It made him anxious in a way he couldn't identify. It might have been just uneasiness or maybe an eagerness to get on with this, to see where it all ended.

***

Topping the long slope brought them to a broad valley where the water gap widened out. Green hills lined either side, rising to give way to a skirt of rocky escarpments hemmed with scrub pines. White shapes dotted the grass. Some of the shapes were moving against the green.

Levon took a pair of binoculars from the pocket of his coat to scan the far hill.

"Sheep?" Ray asked.

"Goats," Levon said. "Let's rein the pack horses here to mark the trail and take a look."

They saddled up, riding just below the brow of a ridgeline to reach the edges of the herd. Fifty or more goats, nannies and billies, took little interest in their approach. A few stopped grazing long enough to blink at the newcomers with their weird eyes. Most just kept feeding, heads down.

A tent in a camo-pattern was staked at the edge of the pines. They dismounted and Ray unshipped his Henry from its scabbard. Levon left his rifle in place on his saddle.

"No dog," Ray said as they dismounted.

"I noticed that too," Levon said.

A figure stepped from the tent to stand in the shade of a fly slung before the entrance flap.

Levon raised a hand in greeting. The figure under the fly answered with a tentative wave.

As they got closer the figure stepped into the sunlight. It was a kid, maybe fourteen or younger, in a wrangler jacket and hoodie. A Denver Broncos ball cap was worn back off a head of thick black hair. Sneakers on his feet. Ray loosened his grip on the rifle.

Levon handed off the reins of his horse to Ray and stepped closer to the boy whose eyes shifted between them both. Ray listened as the pair talked but could not follow any of it. His boss started with a few questions to which the boy shook his head. With the fourth question the boy nodded and replied in a language Ray could not understand. Levon dug in a pocket and came up with a Payday bar that he offered the boy. They spoke some more as the boy took the bar and ripped off the wrapping. He took a bite of the bar and offered the next to Levon who declined. The boy pointed off to the north, speaking animatedly as he chewed.

They said their farewells, leaving the kid to lick the wrapper as they led their mounts back down where the packys stood waiting.

"What did he say?" Ray asked.

"His family lives just north of here, a klick or two," Levon said as they walked. "His father sent him up here with the herd for fresh grazing. He says six families live over there. They've been here nearly five years raising goats and farming off the grid."

"They illegals?"

"Not according to him. He says the government put them here."

"What language were you speaking? It for sure wasn't Spanish."

"Pashto," Levon said.

28

Ed Teal stepped from his office into the Bel-Mar lobby. He was a young man in his early twenties. He effected a western look of yoke shirt, jeans and lizard skin boots despite a distinct back-east accent. At the sight of the two young girls at the reception desk, he put on what he believed passed for charm.

"You the ladies Stu called about?" Ed said, flashing teeth.

"I'm Beth. This is Serena," Merry lied.

"I'm Eddie." He turned to the receptionist. "Kathy, are they all signed in?"

"Yep," Kathy said and handed over visitor stickers that the girls stuck to their jackets.

"Well, come on and I'll show you what we do here," Ed said, holding a swinging door open for them.

The facilities beyond the door were immaculately clean with tiled walls floor to ceiling. The strong smell of disinfectant hid a muskier odor. The broad corridor led to a large room lined with long steel tables at which dozens of workers in white coats and gloves and hairnets worked wrapping cuts of meat that came down conveyors. Men at the end of the conveyors loaded the wrapped cuts into boxes set on pallets. A forklift carried the pallets to another part of the plant. Merry noted that most were Hispanic women. Hope pulled her jacket closed.

"Cold in here, huh?" Ed said, grinning. He pulled a lined coat from a peg and slipped it on. "The whole building is refrigerated to forty degrees. Gets even colder over this way."

He led them through a curtain of plastic strips into a deep room where carcasses hung from hooks suspended below a rail system. The air was frigid, most surfaces covered with a rime of frost. There were hundreds of sides of meat here, horses, ponies, even a few foals.

Hope looked away. Merry kept her voice level.

"Where are they butchered?"

"That's in Building Three," Ed said, his smile more fixed now. "But you ladies don't want to see that. Heck, I don't like going over there myself unless I have to."

"What about the corrals?" Merry said.

"I guess we can walk past them," Ed said and led them between the ranks of hanging meat for a door at the rear.

They stepped into the morning sun and crossed a broad area of gravel and mowed weeds where rows of truck trailers stood parked.

"This for school?" Ed asked. "The guard didn't say. This for a report or something?"

"Something like that," Merry said, not elaborating.

The other side of the trucks they came to the high wooden fences the girls had seen when driving up to the plant. Heavy planks nailed to cross pieces strung between concrete posts. There were gaps of a few inches between each upright. An asphalt drive ran between two of the twenty acre enclosures. They walked along this, the fences rising eight feet in height either side. Hope went to one side to peer through the gap in the boards. Merry joined her.

Inside the enclosure they could see horses milling about. All sizes and colors. Paints, duns, buckskins and dapples. Some had brands visible, others not. A few looked sickly, ribs showing, and hides crisscrossed with the white scars of brush burns. Most were healthy enough even if they were showing some age.

From their restricted aspect they only see a few dozen of the hundreds of animals probably enclosed there.

"Can we go inside?" Merry asked.

"What?" Ed said, confused at first. "Why would you want to do that?"

"Can we?" Hope asked.

"No way. Heck, no. There's insurance and all that shit. Mr. Melnick would have my ass if I let the two of you go wandering in there."

Hope began to protest until Merry grabbed her arm.

"How long do you keep horses penned?" Merry asked.

"From the time they're delivered?" Ed said. "They need to stay corralled until the blood tests come back. That's the law."

"Tests for what?" Merry wasn't curious but felt a need to keep up pretending this was for a school paper.

"Tetanus. Distemper. Glanders. The state makes us test them and the folks buying them on the hoof need blood reports for export."

"So, if a horse came in yesterday, it would still be penned?"

"Yeah. With the weekend we won't be rendering Section One for another two days."

"And this is Section One? Merry asked, pointing to the right.

"Naw. That one," Ed said and nodded to the left.

"Thank you for the tour," Merry said.

"Okay, then. Hope you got enough for your assignment," Ed said, his cool returning. "I'll see you back to the lot."

Back in the El Camino, Merry pulled past the guard house with a friendly wave.

"What will we do, Merry?" Hope said. "Are we just going to drive away?"

"For now."

"But we did not get to see all the horses."

"We will. Tonight. But first we have to go someplace."

"Where?" Hope asked.

"Get on your phone," Merry said. "Find me the nearest hardware store."

29

"Afghans?" Ray said. "Like from Afghanistan?"

"That's the place," Levon said. "They're Pashtuns."

"And you speak their language."

"I spent some time there."

They rode in the direction the boy pointed. The trail they'd followed from the ranch led the same way. The land rose sharply, cut deep with swales and washes where snow melt came down seeking lower ground in the spring. The draws were bone dry now and treacherous riding. They dismounted to lead the mounts up the scree to a wide table land that appeared to run flat toward a fringe of pine woods all around. The rock face of the mountains was in shadow now as the late afternoon sun moved behind them. The ground was better for riding here, sage and light brush, so they mounted up once more to lead the pack animals ahead.

"The kid said they've been here for years," Ray said as they rode easy. "I thought we only left Afghanistan at the beginning of the year."

"They've been relocating friendlies for years,"

Levon said. "Maybe not exactly friendlies. Allies, anyway. Anyone who helped us made themselves an enemy of the Taliban. In some regions, we never really got control away from the Taliban. The government brought some of the locals who helped us here to the US. There was no place safe in their country for them."

"And they dropped them off way out here? I thought the *red man* got a shitty deal from the feds."

"Believe it or not, they're probably just as happy here as they were back home. Happier even without their neighbors shooting at them. There's parts of Helmand Province that don't look all that much different than right here."

They came to the edge of the brush to a place where grass had been recently cut down. Rolls of hay taller than a man sat where they'd been baled. A New Holland hay baler sat in the field. Beyond that they could see metal rooftops behind a stacked stone wall. White smoke rose from a few places.

"We just gonna ride in there like this?" Ray said, looking for signs of life among the distant buildings.

"We'll take it slow. Let them get a good long look at us," Levon said. "Let them think we're just two guys out doing some off-season hunting."

"You think they saw the horse thieves?"

"I can guarantee it. I can almost guarantee our horses are corralled up ahead."

"Then what do we do about it?"

"We don't do shit." Levon turned to fix Ray with a hard look. "Even if we do see our stock. We keep our mouths shut. Especially you."

"Like I speak Afghan."

"Chances are some of these folks were translators.

They'll understand anything you say so don't say anything."

Through a gap in the stone curtain wall, they could see the village. The wall had been constructed within the past few years. Cinderblock buildings of one story painted white lay beyond it. Metal rooftops. An open Quonset hut painted in peeling khaki. There were outdoor ovens built of brick. The white smoke they'd seen was rising from the chimney of one of these. A dog barked somewhere out of sight among the buildings and was silenced.

"Looks government built. Maybe an old forestry encampment," Levon said.

Ray could feel eyes on him though he couldn't see a living soul anywhere.

"You know in the old movies where the white guy rides alone into the Indian camp?" Ray said.

"Like John Wayne?" Levon said.

"Now I know how he felt."

Inside the curtain wall was a one-acre corral of posts and planks backed with hurricane fencing. Within it were a dozen or more horses watching the strangers ride in. At a glance, Ray picked out Flame and Tommy as well as the big black named Charlie and the younger Holman girl's horse.

"Mr. Holman?" Ray said.

"I saw them," Levon said. "Stop looking and shut up."

They continued on at a walk down the main lane toward the collection of buildings. Some men, six bearded adults and four or five teens, stepped from the Quonset to approach the newcomers. Even from a distance Ray could tell these weren't Idahoans. They wore loose fitting clothes that looked like pajamas layered over with long vests. One wore a camo fatigue tunic. They all wore a kind of loose beret-looking hat except for one in an incongruous straw cowboy hat. A few of the younger men sported jeans and jerseys but wore round brimless caps you'd never see at the Walmart. There were no guns he could see. And not a single female, woman or girl, anywhere in sight.

"I'm gonna ask permission to dismount," Levon said. "Get down when I do and, if you have a poker face, start wearing it."

Ray nodded as he tried to remember what all those white guys in the movies did to make it to the end credits.

30

Fresh out of a hot shower, Lew Dollinger lay naked on the bed of his motel room. He tabbed the remote to go twice around the horn on the flat screen mounted above the pressed wood dresser.

No porn. Not even Cinemax. The hottest thing he could find in the middle of the afternoon was a big-titted spokesmodel selling gaudy jade necklaces. He switched to an old TV western and turned the sound down.

At fifty-eight bucks a night the Motel 6 was still no bargain. But his dwindling funds didn't allow for indulgence. And there was no way he was swiping that black card the Chinaman gave him. And try as he might at a local tap room, no ladies invited him home for a tickle and breakfast. Made him homesick for Florida.

Christ on a cross, Idaho was a big-ass place. He'd pulled into Carey the day before after a long ride through a whole lot of nothing to see. There weren't many people here, but they were damned sure spread wide in every direction. He asked around the local businesses after a single dad with two girls who might have moved in recently. There wasn't much in the way of cooperation. For all the howdys he'd gotten since he crossed the Continental Divide, not a living soul had much time for ol' Lew once he started asking questions. Hell, the state motto should be None Of Your Fucking Business. They should put it on the license plates. Bunch of cowboy-hat wearing social retards.

So, he drank a little more than he should. Talked a little more than he ought to. Got his ass thrown out of a place called the Little Wood. He came back to the room and crashed until waking up way past noon with a head that felt like it belonged on someone else's shoulders.

The shower helped some, but he was still wobbly. He decided that he'd write this day off. The two-week deadline was creeping closer but how in God's name would they find him now? He was way off from the last place they could locate him. Unless the tidy little gook had some kind of psychic on the payroll Lew figured he'd bought himself some time. He'd earned a day to fuck off. He was paid up two days in this cracker box and needed a breather. Tomorrow he'd be back on the hunt, poking here and there for a lead on Cade.

Bored, he picked up his phone and stroked the screen to life. Google Maps was up and so was his photo gallery. He touched the gallery and scrolled through, recalling some nasty shots he took of one of the ladies he'd bedded back in Punto Gordo. If he squinted just right, they might be enough to make his pecker hard.

He swiped and swiped, scrolling past the pictures

he took of the Cade farm. The barn. The work shed. All the rooms in the house.

His finger paused at a picture of the living room. He touched the phone with thumb and index finger and parted them to enlarge the image. The two bookcases filled the screen. He zoomed in as much as he could to read the spines of the books. Turning the phone sideways, he was able to make out titles and authors.

Lew turned on his side to snatch the note pad and pen from the nightstand and began making a list.

***

"Harry Potter. You're serious," the snippy little bitch behind the library counter said.

"That's the name on the book, ma'am," Lew said. "Written by Jay Kay Roh-lins."

"I know the author's name," she said. He sensed she bit her tongue not to add 'dumbass.'

"So, you can help me?"

"Help you find two little girls who read Harry Potter."

"Their mama's awful worried about them." Lew had presented her with one of his old business card from when he was a deputy.

"You'd have better luck finding a little girl who *hasn't* read Harry Potter."

"Well, what about some of these others here?" Lew said, unfolding the piece of Motel 6 note paper that he'd written his list on.

The librarian scanned the paper through her reading glasses.

"E. B. Sledge. Don't know that one. Douglas Freeman. Mickey Spillane? You're sure?"

"They're big readers. You have any of those books?"

"If we do. They're in the fiction section."

"And you have records of what book's been taken out and who took 'em?"

"We do, sir." She said 'sir' like she'd say 'shithead.' "But I'm not at liberty to share those names with you."

At liberty?

"Not even to help these poor children get back home to their mother? Their daddy took off with them and he's a dangerous man. God alone knows—"

"Then it shouldn't be any trouble for you to acquire a warrant. You do that and you'll find me most cooperative." The bitch tilted her head like a curious bird as she handed back his list.

"Well, I believe that's exactly what I'll do," Lew said aping her smug smile. "You'll see me shortly with the proper legal papers."

He turned for the door to cross the lobby from the desk. He turned back as he reached the exit to see the bitch was occupied with another customer, some old Jew-looking bastard with a stack of books in his arms.

Lew ducked between two shelves and unfolded his list. He strolled along the rows of bookshelves, always staying out of the line of sight of the main desk. The fiction section was at the rear of the building. He stooped, turning sideways, neck craned to look for the names of authors on the list.

After a brief search he came across one. Alistair MacLean. There were a few well-read paperbacks, some with spines repaired with tape and the author's name re-written by hand. Some were bound in new laminated covers. A few of the titles seemed familiar to him even though they weren't on the list.

He opened a book called *Force Ten from Navarone* and flipped to the back. There was a library card in a manila pouch glued to the inside back cover. It described the history of this book, a record of years of withdraws and returns. Sometimes the book went unread for long periods. The longest being the last as this paperback sat unwanted on this shelf for close to sixteen years.

Until it was taken out and returned just three months prior by Jodie Holman, her name written in a neat schoolgirl hand at the bottom of the yellowing card.

31

After asking if they might pay a visit, Levon and Roy dismounted in the center of the village before the open Q-hut. The men stepped into the sunlight to greet the newcomers. A Kubota tractor sat in the shadows. Bales of fresh hay lined either wall.

The oldest, a man with a wind burnt face dark as teak and fringed in a snow-white beard, took the lead. He offered his hand to Levon who took it in a firm shake. Each man came closer to shake Levon and Ray's hand in turn. A younger man, maybe in his forties, by Levon's estimation, introduced himself as Zalmai Babrak Shinwari. He was son to the white bearded man who was headman of this village. Three of the younger men were Zalmai's sons.

Levon asked after the health of the headman and the rest of his people.

The headman answered that all were well, praise God, and the summer had been good to them with a rich season of grass and many new healthy goat kids born to their herd.

Zalmai asked after Levon's family and Levon

pointed off to the south to indicate where his family lived. He told them that his uncle was roughly the age of Zalmai's father and still quite fit. He had two daughters as well and they were fine young women still in school. He introduced Ray, who nodded dumbly, as a family friend.

After some more small talk, Levon and Ray were invited to share some tea with the men. Levon accepted for them both. Two of the young men led their horses into the shade of the Q-hut where they hitched them to a rail. Ray watched the horses being taken from them, his Henry and his boss's rifle still slung from their saddles. Levon nudged him to follow the men into a low-walled courtyard behind one of the block buildings. They took seats at a trio of picnic tables that surrounded a fire pit. Levon took his binoculars from his coat pocket and set them on the tabletop before him.

Zalmai's sons trotted off to one of the houses and returned with teapots, mugs and a tray of thickly cut bread slices smeared with butter. Ray was handed a mug with the Smokey Bear logo on it. The tea was poured, strong and sweet and Zalmai spoke to Levon.

"We have few visitors," he said. "And few who speak Pashto as well as you."

"I have been to the lands of the Hindu Kush and the deserts of Herat and other places."

"You are a soldier then."

"I was a soldier. I am no longer. My wars are done."

"My oldest son was a soldier with the 209th Corps."

"At Mazar-i-Sharif. I served alongside them for

six months. Your son is no longer with us?"

"Sadly, no. He fell in battle as so many of our village had. I myself served as a translator at Camp Leatherneck until six years ago."

"Was Dan Yoo the general then?"

"He was. I was on his staff. There were many reprisals against my people. My village was most remote and could not be defended. We asked to be relocated. We were in a camp near Kabul for more than two years. It was colder there than in our home in Baghran. We lost some of our oldest and youngest there in the snows. My father made our case to any who would listen. Your state department treated us as pariahs, as dogs to be forgotten. They did not remember how we helped them stand against the Taliban. We were taken from one place of danger only to starve in another."

Levon nodded his sympathy. The elder put a hand to his heart at his son's words.

"It was not until the story of our suffering was seen on Australian television that anyone would listen to us. We were given special immigration visas, all of us. We were grateful to be welcomed to the United States and flown to Tampa in Florida where we stayed in barracks for nearly half a year. My father asked if we could be taken to a place more like our home. And so, they brought us here."

"What was this place before it became your home?"

"It had been a study center for your department of interior." Those last words were in English. The Pashtun had learned a lot in their crash course in government bureaucracy. "It is a good place for us. The grass is rich and the water plentiful much of the year. It is very much like home."

"We had no idea you were up here," Levon said. "Ray and I were after deer and thought this would be virgin hunting ground. We did not expect to find anyone living here in the mountains. A boy tending goats pointed the way."

Levon offered all this without request. It would have been rude for the men to ask him his business. It would have been equally rude for him not to reveal his reasons for being on their land.

"That is Kwazhun, my brother's boy with the herd," Zalmai said. One of the bearded men looked up at the mention of his son's name.

"It looks to me like you thrive here, far from war and trouble," Levon said, looking about the collection of white-washed buildings.

"We do, praise God," Zalmai said. Many of the older men touched hands to their chests. "Your country has been generous."

"You ask little in return for your sacrifices," Levon said, a hand to his own heart. "I am humbled by your hospitality."

"All we have is yours as our guest," Zalmai said with a fixed smile. "You may stay with us tonight, share our evening meal and depart in the morning refreshed."

"That is very generous, Zalmai Shinwari. I wish to thank you and your father, but I have already been away too long from my home. We must start out to return before it is dark."

"Understood. Understood." Zalmai's smile became less practiced, more genuine. He turned to two of the boys seated at another table and barked an order. They trotted off to the Q-hut to retrieve the horses.

The headman rose first, and Levon stood to take his hand once more. A new round of handshakes and well wishes began before they made their way to where the two boys stood holding the reins of the horses. Ray touched Levon's arm.

"Your binoculars, Mr. Holman," Ray said, nodding back toward the tables where the binoculars still sat where Levon had placed them.

"A gift," Levon said. "Bad manners not to leave one. Worse manners to offer it directly."

They both mounted and bowed their heads before turning the horses back the way they'd come. The men and boys bowed their heads as well, hands to hearts.

Neither speaking, they rode along the fence line of the corral as they left. Ray looked to the four captive horses in his peripheral before turning his head to look back at their hosts. The men stood in a group, all silently watching the two guests ride off into the sunset.

"Maybe you can tell me what all of this is about now," Ray said as they moved through the gap in the curtain wall leading the pack animals behind them.

"I don't have all the answers, but I can tell you one thing," Levon said. "Those men are scared."

32

"They didn't look scared to me," Ray said.

"They invited us to stay the night. I refused. They didn't insist." Levon said. He turned his horse down a bank that led to a broad alluvial plain lined by scrub pines either side.

"And that means they're scared? Like a guilty conscience?"

"They didn't steal my horses. They were scared *for* us. The last thing they want is trouble.

"I don't get it. Trouble? You saw the horses. Who stole them?"

"The men they're afraid of." Levon turned his head as he rode, eyes sweeping the rocks above them.

"You're freaking me out," Ray said.

"Good. Stay that way."

They picked their way through the stubby pines and brush to the floor of the plain, a triangular dry riverbed that led like a funnel to the water gap to the south. Thick chaparral covered the far slope all the way to the base of a rock wall. They both dismounted at the bottom of the bank.

"We're not going back the same way we came," Ray remarked, leading his mount and pack horse onto the silty soil.

"That's right. There's no way around the chokepoint ahead though."

"Not without a three-day ride around the escarpment."

"And we're out of radio range here."

"You think maybe Wes or your dad might come looking for us?"

Levon brought his horses to a stop and scanned the banks before answering. He stepped back to pull his rifle from its pack to sling it under one arm.

"Not if they do as they were told. Let's follow the left bank." Levon led his mount and packy under an overhead spread of elders and firs growing along the slope above.

"Is it okay to admit that I'm scared now?" Ray said, looking to the high rocks for some sign of whatever Levon was looking for

"Only way to be. Let's be quiet now."

"Yes, sir."

They moved under the dense shadows of the trees, following the plain as it narrowed toward the cleft.

***

The soft, level alluvial soil allowed them to continue on even as full dark fell on them. There was little danger of any of their mounts breaking a leg in a chuckhole or going lame on sharp rocks. They walked the mounts at an easy pace, stopping only to offer them a handful of sweet feed and a bucket of water. Levon and Ray split the last sandwich between them. Levon crouched on the sand as he ate, studying the way ahead. They were well past the place to the east where they'd passed the boy and the goat herd. It felt like days before rather than hours.

The sides of the dry bed were closing in either side to form a coulee. It was a narrow gully cut through the backslope of the cuesta they'd climbed earlier in the day. Ray could see the walls of the gap ahead standing like bookmarks, black against a star-filled sky. This was the narrow passage, the perfect ambush. If whatever the boss was anticipating was going to happen, it would be there.

Levon moved closer to him and spoke in a low tone that the wind through the pines and gorse would conceal.

"I'm going through first leading both re-mounts," Levon said. "Once I'm out of sight you give it a slow hundred count and follow."

Ray nodded, mouth dry as ash. After a slap to his shoulder, his boss rose and took the reins and lead lines and made for the dark cleft. Ray unshipped his Henry and held it at his side to watch the boss vanish into the shadows of the notch. He started his count, losing his place a few times as he strained his eyes against the night. After a deep breath he resumed the count at twenty, making himself take it slow.

At one hundred, he gave the reins a tug. The chestnut followed him toward the mouth of the coulee. The floor of the channel was twenty feet across with high walls ten feet in height or more in spots. The inclines of the walls were sheer, unclimbable. He stepped the horse over some dead brush that had fallen when the ground above gave way to erosion.

Ray wondered for the first time if the boss might

be using him for bait. If that were the case his boss would have sent him through first with the remounts.

The ground sloped down sharply, and he walked close alongside the horse, a reassuring hand to its neck. As the alluvial bed dropped, the banking walls fell away. He was through the canyon and onto the gentle front slope of the cuesta choked with berry bushes and dwarf pines.

A blinding light from above turned midnight to noon. A popping sound followed to echo off the rocks. His horse shied back at the sudden brilliance. Ray tightened his grip on the reins and put a shoulder to the horse's flank. The weight of the big animal pressed back hard forcing him to jump clear. He was punched to the ground to fall sprawling even as the chestnut collapsed on the sand.

Ray was fighting hard for breath. The horse was down, a high squealing whinny rising from it as it tried to rise kicking. He was aware now of sounds all around him. The crack and whine of rifles far off and tracer rounds too near. Closer, louder, was the bark of an automatic weapon. Green tracers arced from somewhere in the brush toward the high rocks off the left. He rolled on his side, gasping at a lancing pain that ran from his right side down his leg.

The parachute flare drifted behind some scrub to throw crazed shadows across the coulee mouth. Ray clawed at the sand for the nearest shadows, wondering where his rifle had gotten too. His right arm was numb now. He couldn't remember ever feeling this exhausted. He fought the urge to rest his head on the cool earth.

A shadow fell over him. A hand took the neck of

his coat and shirt in an iron grip. He was dragged, belly-down into some brush, thorns scratching his face and poking through his jeans.

Levon set him upright against the lee of a shallow gully.

"I'm shot," Ray said.

Levon set his rifle aside to pull open Ray's coat. Blood shone black where it stained the pullover.

"Let me see your eyes," Levon said and studied Ray's face.

"I'm gonna die, right?"

Levon said nothing, tearing off his own coat. With a buck knife, Levon slit the side of the hoodie, work shirt and tee until he was down to Ray's bare ribs. There was a deep bruise along the ribs on Ray's right side. He felt around the boy's back to look for any wounds. He lifted Ray forward to tie the sleeves of his coat around the chest. Ray grunted as the knot was drawn tight.

"I'm gonna die, right?" Ray said again, weaker this time.

"That's up to you," Levon said. "If you feel like sleeping, don't."

"How bad is it?"

"You're not shot, Ray. You have a couple of broken ribs. I think maybe your horse kicked you when you were falling."

"Hurts when I breathe in," Ray nodded.

"You're not in shock but that could come." Levon handed him a water jug. "Can you hold on awhile by yourself?"

Ray nodded; lips pressed tight.

"You keep pressure on your side, don't move around and don't let that knot slip. Take sips of that water."

"I lost my rifle," Ray said.

"Here." Levon produced a shiny black automatic from somewhere and placed it in Ray's hand before rising to a crouch and picking up his rifle.

"Where you going?" Ray asked.

"To get our asses out of here," Levon said before vanishing into the dark.

33

Black shadows pooled between the silver trunks of the birches under an overcast sky. Merry led the way through them, carrying a canvas gear bag by a strap. Hope followed her, long-handled bolt cutters balanced over her shoulder. A drizzling rain had awakened a million toads. Their chirruping wafted and waned in a lazy rhythm all around the girls as they followed a trail through the dark. After twenty minutes, they could see the lights of the Bel-Mar plant through the trees.

They crouched in the brush at the edge of a field of milkweed. The cyclone and razor wire fence ran straight across the clearing with a mown strip behind. Beyond that was the plank fencing of the corrals.

Merry and Hope listened for any sounds from the plant. They settled in place to watch and wait. Merry checked the timer on her phone set for thirty minutes. If there was a regular security patrol it would pass at least twice an hour, given the size of the property.

Hope shivered in the cold despite three layers of clothing topped by one of the black hoodies they bought for this occasion. What Merry called a 'mission.' She stifled a yawn.

They'd parked the El Camino just off a dirt road in the evening to get a few hours' sleep. Hope had slept intermittently, sitting up in the cab with her back to the door and the rolled-up hoodie for a pillow. It had been a long day starting way before dawn with lots of driving. Two hours from home to Bel-Mar. The nearest hardware store was in Arco near the Montana border more than an hour away then an hour back. The highlight was burgers and fries at a place called Lost River.

Merry's hand woke her from a half-dozing state.

"That's a half hour," Merry said. "I think the place is closed for the night. No security patrols."

Hope nodded and followed her sister into the waist-high milkweed.

At the fence they pulled on heavy canvas gloves. Hoods up and cloth masks on their faces, Hope thought they looked like ninjas she'd seen in some of Uncle Fern's movies. Merry cut the metal rings that attached the cyclone fencing to the bottom cross rail and from one of the upright posts. Hope pulled on the fencing while Merry cut wires near the upright. Together they pulled on the wire, folding it back to make an opening tall enough and wide enough to lead a horse through. Merry secured the cut end in place with plastic tie wraps to keep their new doorway open.

They crossed onto the plant property and approached the corral fences. Merry felt the tension in her neck and shoulders subside as they reached the wooden fence. There were no motion-detector lights. She'd already looked for cameras. Rustlers did not expect to be rustled, apparently.

Merry took a pry bar from the gear bag and set the tooth end behind one of the upright slats. The ten penny nails squealed in protest as she heaved the handle of the bar to her again and again. She and Hope froze, breath held. The amphibious chorus in the woods went uninterrupted so Merry pulled again and the bottom of a board came free. She set the pry against the next board and worked it loose.

Working together the girls gripped the bottom of each board and wiggled them back and forth until they came away from the cross bar above their heads. The boards dropped out of place, and they let them fall to the grass. They freed the next two boards, only loosening them at the top but leaving them in place.

Merry stepped one foot through the narrow gap they'd made. She started at finding ten or more horses standing and watching her in silence. Their ears were forward and snouts twitching at their surprise visitor.

"Come on," Merry whispered. Hope joined her.

They snapped on penlight flashlights. Merry pointed to the right and Hope moved off, her hand over the end of the flash to hide its glare. Merry made her way to the left. The once curious horses lost interest as they realized the visitors did not bring them anything to eat.

The horses parted as she moved through the herd. Some were on the ground. Most were up on their hooves. The ground was soddened in places with puddles of standing urine. Merry's boots squelched through a swamp of manure, disturbing clouds of flies. The scent of horse droppings had never bothered her before. Here, in this enclosed place with hundreds of animals, the powerful funk was making her head swim. The number of horses and the stink was overwhelming her.

It was surreal to be alone among so many of another species. As much as Merry loved horses, she respected them. They could be dangerous. And a herd this size, if riled or scared, could be absolutely murderous. Anything could set one of them off and the rest would share the panic. Merry began to regret separating from Hope.

***

The penlight in one hand, Hope maneuvered between the horses on the other side of the corral, cooing to them in a low sing-song voice a lullaby her mother sang to her and her siblings.

> *Que llueva, que llueva,*
> *la Virgen de la Cueva,*
> *los pajaritos cantan,*
> *las nubes se levantan*

A gentle hand to a neck to urge a mare aside was answered by a nuzzle to her hooded head. Hope turned to a horse studying her with black, unblinking eyes. A quarter horse in dappled gray with black stockings. A year old. Certainly, no more than two years. It nipped the cloth of her hood with rubbery lips. The mare wore a rope bridle of braided cloth striped in shades of blue. Hope give the muzzle a gentle pat before turning to continue her search for their stolen horses.

The mare followed her, keeping pace as she worked through the horses. Each time she stopped she felt the animal's head give her a prod in the back. Hope pulled her facemask down to clamp the penlight in her lips, leaving a hand free to take the mare by the rope bridle. Together they moved deeper into the gathered animals.

***

Merry reached the part of the corral nearest the plant buildings. She could see the roofs of the packing building and abattoir over the top of the fence. She called for Hope in a hushed voice. Her sister approached from within the herd leading a dappled gray on a rope lead.

"What are you doing?" Merry said in a whisper.

"She followed me," Hope said with a shrug.

"We're looking for *our* horses," Merry said, annoyed.

"I have not seen them. Have you?"

"No, but we could have missed them."

"I called Felicity's name," Hope said. "She always comes when I call her."

"She always comes because you have a feed bucket in your hand when you call her," Merry said, impatient.

"I'm taking her with us," Hope said and tugged the lead, so the mare followed her along the fenceline back the way they came.

"How do we get her back?" Merry said, walking alongside. "Are you going to ride her home?"

"If I have to."

"That's stupid."

"You're stupid."

"This wasn't the plan?" Merry said.

"What was the plan? If we found our horses here, how were we going to get them home?"

Merry gave up. There was no budging her little sister when she got an idea like this in her head. Not when it came to animals anyway. She put Hope's unreasonable insistence down to stress and exhaustion. They'd both been more than a little freaked by the theft of the horses. Now her little sister's fear and anger were taking the form of pity for this spirited gray. The mare was awfully sweet, Merry admitted, and didn't deserve to wind up on some Frenchman's dinner plate. But then, neither did any of these other animals.

Also, she had no answer for the unassailable logic of Hope's question. What *were* they going to do if they found horses they were looking for?

They reached the breach they'd made in the fence and had to shoo away a big gelding who was sticking his head through the boards to munch weeds. Merry went through first and yanked the last two boards free to make a gap wide enough to allow the mare through.

The girls moved at a trot for the hole in the cyclone fence. Merry carried the tools and gear bag while Hope led the mare. A sharp whinny made them turn. A horse, that big gelding, was through the wooden fence now with two other horses stamping and nipping to be the next ones through.

Hope pulled down on the bridle to draw the mare's head down to snap on a lead line and backed up, leading her through the gap. Once on the other side of the wire fence, the girls looked back to see that a half dozen horses had made their way out of the corral with more following. Some were content to graze on fresh grass. Others were running, tails up and heads high through the rain, following the cyclone fencing toward the main yard of the plant. The section of fencing where the girls had removed the planking was leaning outward now under the weight of the horses pressing together to get free of the corral.

"See what you started?" Merry said.

34

Levon dropped to the ground as a second flare exploded to light up the night. He noted its position before pressing his eyes closed to preserve night vision. It dropped short of the previous flare somewhere to the east, closer to the source of the rifle fire.

He remained still, unseeing but listening. The horses had run clear out of range except for the chestnut that lay dying at the opening of the coulee. Its irregular breathing had a wet sound as its lungs filled with blood.

No more rifle fire. They'd be watching for movement. Maybe taking advantage of the blinding light to move closer. The rifles were AKs. He knew the sound as well as he knew Merry's voice.

He should have let Ray go first. The ambushers knew there were two of them and didn't drop the hammer until the second of them came into sight. But then, Levon wouldn't have been in position to offer suppression fire.

Ray's injury wasn't a danger unless he had a

punctured lung. The danger now was shock and exposure. That started the clock. He had until daybreak at the latest to get them both out.

The light through his eyelids turned from red to gray and he opened his eyes away from the last direction of the flare. It had dropped sizzling to the ground somewhere out of sight behind a berm.

There were three of them, maybe more. And they had three options. Sit where they were and snipe at available targets. Come down and finish them off at close range. Wait them out until morning.

Levon thought the second option was the most likely. The draw to come down to where the chestnut lay dying would be irresistible. Maybe they were professional enough to resist their own impatience to see Levon and Ray dead. They were either military trained or just armed thugs. That would be all the difference.

That would all depend on who they were. Levon had a general idea of what kind of men were shooting at him from the dark. There was still a range of possibilities. They could be punk kids. But their actions suggested some degree of arms training. Their equipment as well. Some kind of launcher was being used to send up the flares. To what degree of training they'd had would determine how much of an edge he had on them.

Levon rose in the fresh dark to a crouch and moved off south. They'd be hampered by looking into the light of their own flare. He needed to be anywhere but where they expected him to be if or when they launched a third flare.

Fifty paces south and he shifted course in a shallow arc to the east, keeping placed in his mind where he left Ray. Moving as quickly as he could without making more noise than he could help, he followed a curving trail that brought him to a place between the ambushers' position on the rock and the place where his ranch hand lay wounded. He dropped to his belly to listen.

There was nothing to hear but the wind whispering through the grass tops. He concentrated his hearing to listen through the white noise of the shifting stalks. Levon closed his eyes. His world became the aural landscape around him. His mind searched for anomalies, sounds out of place.

An electronic hiss, muffled and brief, followed by a hushed voice. It was somewhere between him and the rocks rising to the east. A radio. They'd sent someone, or more than one someone, down from their hide on a recon.

Levon shifted to lie on his side and slid his own radio from the holder on his belt. He retrieved earbuds from his shirt pocket and plugged them in. Eyes toward the sound of the squelch and reply, he twiddled the dial, hunting along the frequency settings.

On his third choice a voice came alive in his ear. A male voice speaking in Pashto. The poor audio quality and the man's hushed tones made it hard to determine his age. There was a quickness to his voice brought on by the rapid breathing of an adrenaline rush. This was the man closest to him. He was assuring someone that he could see nothing. A voice, calmer and clearer, urged him to look closer.

"Maybe they are waiting," the man nearest Levon said.

He was perhaps twenty yards or less from Levon's

position. There would be no more flares as they would expose both hunter and prey. Levon locked eyes on the general direction he guessed the man to be.

"Maybe they are dead," the stronger voice said.

"We should wait until morning."

"Wait for what?"

"The birds. The birds will come if they are dead, and we will know."

"The birds will come anyway to feed on the horse."

"Why do you not come look for them?"

"Who is oldest?"

Levon rose to a crouch once more to creep forward. He moved slowly so as not to disturb the grass stalks. Rather than a direct path, he chose an arc that would bring him behind where he suspected the man to be hiding. The conversation continued in his ear.

"Reveal yourself. See if they fire at you."

"You should stand up," the whisperer said.

"If they shoot at you, we will know where they are. We will shoot and kill them."

Two or more were up in the rocks. The scout was on his own. There was a long pause of radio silence.

"Can you hear me, Asfand?" It was either the scout's name or an insult meant to motivate him. Asfand meant hero.

Silence in the earbud as Levon lowered himself to the ground. He pulled the piece from his ear to listen to the night. He unslung his M4 and set it beside him.

"I hear you."

The words came from somewhere ahead. Less than ten feet from where Levon launched himself to his feet.

He landed atop the prone figure with the full weight of his body. One hand pulled the man back by a fistful of thick black hair. His other arm snaked around the man's throat. A knee in the small of the man's back, Levon jerked the man toward him, throat clamped tight in the crook of his arm, wrist gripped in his other fist to draw the chokehold closed.

The man struggled under Levon's weight, hands reaching in spasms for the rifle that lay in the dirt just out of reach. Levon pulled harder, feeling bone move on bone in the man's neck. The hands waved useless in the air as he resisted the strangling force with a desperate, feral energy.

The movements became more and more feeble as the pressure starved the man's brain of oxygen. The body went limp beneath Levon, the legs and arms ceasing their struggle. Levon increased the pressure and counted off the time. He felt warm wetness against the knee he had planted between the man's legs. The scent of urine, with a strong element of garlic, reached his nostrils. He kept the pressure on until a count of two hundred before he dropped the lifeless man to the ground.

He turned the man over to rummage through his pockets. Despite the face twisted in the final agonies, a black tongue swollen behind the teeth of a rictus grin, the dead man appeared to be young. No older than twenty-one. Patchy fuzz where he had attempted to grow a beard.

This was one of the boys who brought them their horses back in the village.

Levon came up with two spare magazines in the cargo pocket of an anorak in forest camo. Also, some hash folded in aluminum foil and rolling papers.

A few loose dollars and some change. No kind of identification.

The radio squelched where it lay in the dirt.

"Asfand? Will you do as I say? Will you stand and allow us to kill them?"

"Ishâllâ," Levon said, in a hushed voice that might sound like the dead boy to the listener on the other end.

God willing.

35

A section of corral fencing gave way under the weight of a dozen or more horses trying to press through the opening. The boards fell with a crash. The horses leapt the cross bar to rush along the open grass enclosed by the cyclone fencing. Stirred by either fear or instinct or just basic equine curiosity, they followed the corral fence deeper into the plant.

Only a few trotted to the gap in the wire fence created by Merry and Hope. These followed the girls and the dapple gray they led through the milkweed toward the trees. Merry looked back as the corral emptied of horses that now ran through the rain toward the halo glow of lights from the plant buildings.

She'd seen horses break fences before. But in her experience only one or maybe two rogues would go stray. Here at Bel-Mar the whole herd was breaking out. She thought she knew the reason for this sudden run for freedom. It was days spent smelling the scent of spilled blood in the air, the blood of their own kind. In some way, the animals knew that escape meant survival.

Her breath caught. The plant buildings were thrown into silhouette by a new burst of halogen glare. Someone had become alerted to the escaped horses. Or, more likely, there were motion sensitive lights closer to the plant entrance.

"They know we're here now," Merry said, taking her own grip on the dapple's lead line. "We have to get back to the car."

"They will think the horses got out on their own," Hope said and tugged on the lead line.

"Not once they see the hole we cut." Merry pulled harder to get the lead from her sister's grip. "We have to let this one go."

"No," Hope said with a hoarse whisper.

Merry could hear the tears in Hope's voice. She released the rope line. Merry ran on into the trees following her sister with two horses, a bay and a chestnut trotting behind.

Behind them they could hear the sound of a man's voice calling. A glance back and they could see a blue strobe flashing as a security vehicle moved over the plant yard.

***

"All right," Merry said. "What now?"

The rain was falling harder by the time they reached the El Camino. Hope gripped the lead line of the dappled gray. The two other horses who'd followed were standing beneath the trees, the flesh of their backs shivering where the cold rain fell.

"We can put her in the back," Hope said, nodding to the bed of the El Camino.

"It's not a horse trailer."

"I will ride with her."

"The two of you in the bed? You'd be too heavy."

"Then I ride her," Hope said, leading the mare closer to the car.

"Where?" Merry said.

"That way." Hope pointed to an open field on the other side of the road.

"Home's that way." Merry pointed down the dirt road.

"They will be looking that way." Hope stepped up on the bumper to give her a boost and swung onto the mare's back.

With a deep sigh, Merry took out her phone and found their current location.

"There's a road north of here. Skylark Road." She held the phone up to Hope. "You ride till you reach that and look for me. I'll drive around to meet you."

"And then what?"

"We'll call Daddy, and he can bring the trailer, I guess. If we're not both arrested first."

Hope beamed down from where she sat. She gave the gray a nudge with her heels. The fugitive bay and chestnut followed them across the road at a trot and into grass. Merry watched until they were out of sight in the murkiness of the wet night.

"That girl has zero regard for authority," Merry said to herself. "She's a real Cade now."

36

The men in the rocks saw twin flashes from the floor of the wash. They were followed by two flat pops. Four brighter blooms of light with the deeper boom of .762 rounds coming after. Then silence.

"Asfand? Are you there?" one of the men said into his handset.

Silence. A weak squelch from the radio.

"Asfand? Can you hear me?"

Silence. A hiss. A voice, weak and muted through a sizzle of white noise.

"Yes. I am wounded."

The man with the radio looked to the other who did not turn, eyes intent on the darkness below.

"Are they dead? Are the Americans dead?"

Silence. The voice, weaker than before came through the electric hiss.

"Yes."

"Both?"

"Both dead."

"Keep your radio on, brother. We are coming." The radio man stood, gesturing for the other to rise.

They descended from the rocks on separate paths. Once in the grass they kept fifty paces apart. They approached the place where they saw the early muzzle flashes. Each formed two points of a triangle on a path for the place where they supposed Asfand to be.

Rifles up, fingers on triggers as they had been trained. Eyes focused through the ringed front sight of their rifles as they had been trained. Deep breaths released slowly as they had been trained.

As they neared the place where they would intersect they could hear the squawk of a radio.

"Asfand? Can you hear me?"

The radio man's voice came back to him, clear but tinny, from a place not forty meters ahead. They moved faster now, eager to reach their fallen brother.

The first to reach the radio found it lying alone in a place where the grass had been crushed flat. He stooped to pick it up. He turned to hold the now silent radio up to his comrade.

A shadow rose off to his far right. A star-shaped flame grew there to turn the whole world white.

The other man saw his comrade fall against a corona of triple flashes. He ran away as he had not been trained. Panting and pumping, he sprinted toward the greater dark. A force struck his legs causing him to stumble and fall. His face struck the dirt. His rifle collided with his chest where he fell on it. He thought, at first, he had been physically tackled by the man who killed his comrade except he could feel no weight upon him.

Trying to rise to his knees, he discovered that his legs would not respond. He tried to lever up using the arm trapped beneath him to turn on his side. A booted foot stamped down on his wrist, pinning it against the barrel of his rifle.

"How many are you?" a voice said from above him.

This was not how he was meant to meet God. Tears sprang to his eyes.

"How many are you?" the voice said again.

He held three fingers extended in the dirt.

He went to God weeping.

***

Levon checked Ray's pulse. It was weak but steady.

"I heard shooting," Ray said, his voice tired.

"Nothing to worry about now," Levon said. "Drink some water."

"The horses."

Levon cinched the knotted arms of his coat tighter. Ray bit his lip.

"Don't worry about the horses," Levon said, holding the jug for Ray to take a few swallows. "You won't be riding for a while."

"How we gonna get back?"

"I'll make up a litter. Carry you if I have to."

"That's more than thirty miles."

"I'd call in help, but the radio won't reach. Not until we get the other side of the gap."

"The Afghans."

"Not so sure that's a good idea," Levon said, standing. "Stay awake while I find some wood for that litter."

Levon moved into the brush toward a stand of taller trees hoping to find some fallen boughs there.

From somewhere to the north a rumbling sound reached him. He turned back to where Ray lay against the bank of the draw. A nimbus of light was growing like a false dawn over top of the brush. The rumbling grew louder until the tall shape of a tractor could be seen behind the glare of its headlamps.

Levon dropped to a knee between himself and Ray, rifle raised toward the light. A shadow moved across the brilliance to take the shape of a man. It was Zalmai Babrak Shinwari, walking to them with empty hands raised.

37

It was just after two in the morning when Fern was awakened by the phone ringing. He fumbled for his glasses on the nightstand before searching through the covers for the cordless.

"Merry?"

"She's not there?" Levon's voice on the other end of the phone.

"Her and Hopey took off somewhere before I woke up. Haven't seen them since they went off to bed last night."

"One thing at a time," Levon said. "I need you to get Wes and come to where I am. Tell him to grab the med kit. Get something to write with."

Fern was already in route to the kitchen and found a pen on the counter. He poised it above the back of an envelope he'd plucked from the bill basket.

"Fire away."

"We're at the Robert E. Smylie Department of Land Geological Survey Station. I'm calling you on a landline from there."

"What the hell, Levon?"

"You head east on the county road to Branch Road. You look for a service road off to your left. I don't know how far along. Take that to the end and that's where I am."

"How far is this?"

"Thirty or more miles as the crow flies. And, Fern?"

"Yeah."

"You had one job."

"Hell, nephew. Remember how you and Dale were at her age? The apple don't fall far."

"You tried calling?"

"Of course, I damn sure did. Jesus. She's not answering. Neither of them are."

"We'll talk about it when you get here."

***

Some of the color had returned to Ray's face. He was asleep on a bed in Zalmai's house. He had clean bandages wrapped around his ribs and held in place with clamps.

Levon was assisted by one of Zalmai's daughters who had served at a volunteer hospital in Lashkargah back home in Helmand. The village had a decent supply of medical equipment, mostly US surplus. More of the previously concealed women came forth to provide fresh linens.

Confident that Ray was stable for now, Levon stepped outside where Zalmai and some of the men stood smoking in the dark.

"They are dead?" he asked Levon. "You are certain?"

"They're as dead as they'll ever be. There were three?"

Zalmai nodded, eyes lowered.

"Who were they?"

"Animals. Trash." He offered Levon a cigarette. Levon took the cigarette and allowed Zalmai to light it. He let it burn away in his hand. He was not a smoker but it would be impolite to refuse a gift from his host.

"Not of your tribe?"

"One of them was a cousin of a cousin. They came here in the winter. Two of them. They were unwelcome. But they were armed. They corrupted the boy, the son of one of my brothers. They turned him into one of them with their words."

"Were they part of the Kabul airlift?"

Zalmai shrugged. The other men nodded, pinpoints of light bobbing in the dark.

"We are not refugees," one of them said. "We come here wanting nothing but to be left to ourselves. We bother no one. We ask for nothing."

"And these come," Zalmai said. "To steal. To live like bandits. They talked of jihad. They called us cowards and women. We have no guns. We left that behind to farm in this new country."

"So, what do we do now?" Levon said.

Zalmai looked puzzled. He turned to the other men who muttered among themselves.

"What do we do? What are we to do?" Zalmai asked.

"Do you have contact with anyone outside of here? With the state or anyone federal?"

"There are visits every month from someone from Boise." Zalmai pronounced it Buh-shee. "Not always the same man. Once they sent a woman. Sometimes doctors come. For the children and the old ones."

"Do we tell them about this?"

Zalmai and the men conferred in hushed tones, their backs to Levon. They reached a consensus and Zalmai turned back to Levon.

"We tell nothing. We ask nothing."

Levon nodded, dropping the unsmoked cigarette to the ground and toeing it out. He took Zalmai's hand in his before shaking each man's hand in turn.

***

Fern arrived within the hour, driving the Ford up the gravel service road. He was pulling the horse trailer behind. Wes brought along the toolbox that served as their medical kit and joined Zalmai's daughter in the impromptu hospital room. Ray's vitals were stable enough to give him some morphine for the pain. Wesley joined Levon and Fern around the fire pit where some of the men were sharing a pot of tea. The Pashto watched while the Americans spoke in English.

"Orzala's taking good care of him," Wesley said, accepting a mug.

"First name basis, huh?" Fern said.

"She speaks English and she learned medicine fast back home," Wesley said. "He's out for a few hours. We have to watch for signs of fever. That means a perforated lung. She says it's not a good idea to move him for a few days."

"Can you stay with him, Wes? Till he can be moved?" Levon asked.

"Sure, I can," Wesley said. "But that's not the question. What do we do about all this shit?"

"More bodies to bury," Fern said. "Just like back home."

"That's just it, Ferny," Wesley said, "We can't go back home. And now *this* place is fucked."

"It's got nothing to do with you. Any of you," Levon said. "Worst comes to worst it's me who'll have to take off."

"So, what are we gonna do?" Wesley asked.

"That's up to Ray," Levon said. "When he wakes up."

38

The phone was ringing when Fern opened the door to the house. The landline.

He and Levon had just gotten the four horses off the trailer and into the barn where they were watered and hayed. They'd have to stay in their stalls until the gap in the fence was repaired.

Fern tore the receiver off the kitchen wall phone. It was Merry.

"Uncle Fern, me and Hope are up in Custer County."

"Me and your daddy's been worried sick," Fern began.

"Where is Daddy?"

"He's down at the barn right now. What're you two up to?"

Levon came into the kitchen at a rush and snatched the phone from his uncle's hand.

"Merry," he said.

"We're all right. We're both fine," Merry said, sounding tired. "We just need a little help, is all."

"Are you in trouble?"

"Not at the moment. All's we need is you to come

pick us up."

"The Camino broke down?"

"No. Runnin' fine. We need the horse trailer. For some horses."

"Horses? What horses?"

"Some we found."

"Merry..." Levon began before his daughter cut him off.

"I'm gonna give you the location we're at. Can you drive up here?"

"I can run up there, I guess. Wes can watch the place."

"Did you and Ray find the horses?"

"We did. They're back in the barn." Levon winced at the sound of Merry telling Hope the good news. Squealed celebration until Merry, breathless, got back on the phone.

"All of them?"

It pained him deep to tell her. Only he knew it was the best, the kindest, thing to do to let his little girls know the truth now.

"All but Dusty."

"Did he suffer?" Merry said, her voice small after a long silence.

"It was quick." He spared her any details.

"Better write this down," she said. "You can phone us when you get closer and I'll send you our exact location."

"I'll do that, honey," Levon said after he'd written down the route number and mile marker on the back of an envelope.

"They all right?" Fern said when Levon had hung up.

"Someone answered your prayers, old man," Levon said.

39

Lew Dollinger drove past the mailbox marked HOLMAN just after dawn.

A mile or so farther he made a U turn and looked for places along the road to pull off. He pulled the Tundra off the county road a half mile shy of the mailbox where heavy brush grew along the lip of a drainage ditch. He parked the truck in a dry notch that left it out of sight from the roadway.

From the rear seat he pulled a Playmate cooler containing four cans of Coors and a ham and cheese sandwich on ice. He looped the strap of a pair of binoculars over one shoulder and, after locking up the Tundra, started a climb up a hump of land that he hoped overlooked the Holman place.

It didn't. He continued on down the other side of the berm and walked through tall grass to where the land rose again aways on. With the colorful blue and white cooler, sunglasses and binoculars he looked like he was heading for a ballgame.

The sun was low behind clouds, and it was surprisingly cool for the time of year. Maybe this was what early fall felt like out here. The air was dry and there was a breeze out of the north. Still, this was more exercise than he was accustomed to. He was quickly bathed in sweat under his wifebeater and cotton shirt.

He hoped the long walk would pay off. It had all the looks of a winning ticket. The Jodie Holman name he found on the card in the ancient paperback matched the recent sale of the house and parcel he hoped lay just over the next hill. Six months past, the property was purchased by a Lyle Holman late of Louisiana. An all-cash sale according to the county tax records. There were new accounts with the electric and phone companies under the name Holman. Further investigation into Mr. Holman revealed that he had three vehicles with new state registrations. Two of them had been bought in the past five months and all with cash. No kids were registered at the local school but that meant nothing.

Lew stooped as he trudged near the top of the second hill. He was winded from the climb and bathed in greasy sweat. That first beer would taste good, his reward for his efforts.

At the crest of the hill, he stooped low, a hand bracing him as he crouched to peer through jimson at the rooftops of buildings gleaming silver in the light of the rising sun. A quick scan through the lenses showed nothing moving below. The 30X scopes brought him right into the broad yard before the house. A pole light in front of a barn building winked out as the sky grew brighter. A couple of trucks and an El Camino parked out front. There was a 24-foot travel trailer set apart from the house and a steel roofed carport. A big patch of land was fenced in, the barn forming the corner of a paddock that had to be ten acres or more. Nothing moved there either. If they had livestock it was probably all stabled overnight.

He took a seat on the sandy soil and set the binoculars aside to get himself a breakfast beer. Taking sips of the ice-cold brew to wash down the dry sandwich, he watched the place for any signs of motion. The only thing moving was grasshoppers flitting from one stalk of feed grass to another.

Halfway through his second beer Lew was feeling dozy after his long walk. The hypnotic flitter of grasshopper wings all around him didn't help. One of them landed on his near-bald head starting him from his torpor.

He brushed the insect away with a swat. As he reached for the half-drunk beer, warm now, he could hear voices below. Sounded like kids. And a yapping dog.

Lew turned onto his belly and raised the scopes to his eyes. He trained the lenses toward the source of the voices. The rear doors of the barn were wide open. Some horses were trotting away into the paddock with some kind of little dog running alongside, yipping and barking. He scanned for whoever he'd heard shouting but saw no one.

He watched the barn area with his naked eyes. Ten minutes or so and a tiny pair of figures stepped from the open doorway. He raised the binoculars and focused in on two girls, the taller of the two pushing a full wheelbarrow. The other followed holding some kind of rake by the handle. Twiddling the dial brought the pair into crystal clarity. The taller girl had shoulder-length hair of ashen blonde.

The smaller was darker with ink black hair in a ponytail. Both were in jeans tucked into rubber boots and both appeared to be laughing.

Though he could not hear the words of their exchange, he could tell they were enjoying their work. Shoveling shit and still happy about it. His gaze followed them to one side of barn where the taller girl upended the barrow at the foot of a heap of manure. The younger one used the rake to make sure all the load was dispensed. The little dog returned to the barn to follow them back into the barn. He continued watching as they made two more trips to the shit-pile and then returned to the interior of the barn where they remained.

He spent this interval with his lenses turned toward the house. A male stepped from the travel trailer to walk to the house. Cowboy hat and jeans. From his gait and build he looked to be a young man. Lew stayed with him to the house which he entered without knocking.

The voices of the girls reached him again. The taller of the two had run a hose from a spigot and was filling a concrete trough set twenty feet from the rear wall of the barn. The smaller one, he could see her face now and figured her for a Mexican or something, was calling to the horses with her hands cuffed either side of her mouth. She was calling their names in a high, shrill little girl voice. A few of the horses, he counted seven, interrupted their grazing to canter back for a drink.

The taller girl dropped the end of the hose into the trough and moved at a jog for the fence line. She was looking toward the house. He could hear her voice responding to a call. Lew swung his gaze to follow hers. Two male figures stood in the shade of the house's veranda. The taller of them came down the steps and into the sunlight.

It was the big fucker who sandbagged Lew back in Huntsville. The sumbitch who scared him near shitless. The man the trim little gook was so anxious to get ahold of. The man Rolly Taggart was willing to pay ten grand for dead.

Lew continued watching Levon Cade walk across the gravel to where both girls had reached the fence. He was speaking to them though his voice did not reach Lew's ears. The youngest ended the exchange with a squeal before both girls ran for the barn with the little dog yipping at their heels.

Up in his hide, Lew set the binoculars and poured the last of his lukewarm Coors into the dirt.

"God damn it," he sighed to himself before rising to take the long walk back to his truck.

40

Levon lost sight of the girls at the sale barn and that was all right with him.

They dashed ahead looking into the stalls and pens at the livestock and gear on display. Even though they were no longer looking for horses, visiting the sale each week had become a tradition. They were horse rich now with the addition of the three Merry and Hope brought back from their adventure. Two of those were well past their prime but Levon didn't mind the added expense. Anything to help the girls over the loss of Dusty.

The sale was a place to meet other local ranchers as well as pick up good deals in the many stalls and tents set up to sell tack, gear, liniments, boots, clothing and whatever else might be needed by the horse and cattle folks that dominated the county. It was a countrified mall that made Levon feel at home even though his home was two thousand miles away.

He picked up a box of leather working gloves that he carried back to the Ram. Levon bought himself a coffee and a peppers and egg sandwich and took a seat at one of the rows of picnic tables where they were to meet later. He was content to sip hot coffee and spend the time people watching.

Ray showed up at the food trucks with a pretty redhead who came to his shoulder. She wore faded jeans and a Boise State jersey. She was laughing at something he said and touched his arm as he paid for sodas and fries for the pair of them. Levon turned away to give them their privacy as they walked to a table in the next row and took a seat.

His main hand, his only hand, was on the mend and would be back to regular work in a week or two. Ray had an x-ray at the clinic in Carey that revealed hairline fractures on his right side that were already healing. His injuries were common as sunrise in this part of the country. He'd been thrown by a horse and that was true enough. He'd be wrapped a bit longer but was already walking upright and breathing without much pain.

They'd have to forego putting cattle on the grass until the next calving season. But that would give them time to set up pens and shelter as well as run an irrigation line out into the government land for watering. They'd be back in the spring to start their herd.

Levon was aware of someone sliding into a seat across the table from him. There was always a crowd on sale day, and it wasn't unusual to share a table with another party.

"You're a hard man to locate, Mr. Holman," the newcomer said.

Levon turned to face the man across the table. A pale man with piggy eyes and a crooked smile of amusement twisting his face above a scraggly chin beard. The man's face was red from too much recent sun.

"Lew Dollinger."

"Never forget a face, huh?" Dollinger chuckled dryly. "Don't nobody forget my face, more's the shame."

Levon said nothing.

"Thought this'd be the best place for us to meet. Too many folks around, including your girls."

"What is it you want?"

"You already give me all I can ask for," Dollinger shrugged. "I'm referring to you not killing me back a while."

"Uh huh," Levon said.

"And I can see by your expression you're regretting that decision right about now." Dollinger's grin was turning brittle at the edges.

"Uh huh," Levon said.

"I've had time to wonder why you did that. The theory I like most is that you were just pure D tired of killing. I caught you, or *you* caught *me*, at a bad time for you and good time for me. If you see what I'm saying."

Levon said nothing.

"What brings me out to the west is that you and I have run into some trouble with the same people."

"The law?"

"Not the law, Mr. Holman. Nothing like the law. Some men who want to find you very badly. They want you so bad they let me go free to run you down. Even promised to pay me."

"And you're looking for me to match their bid?"

"Naw. First, you'd never do that. Second, I'm not so sure they won't toss my ass in a ditch right next to yours once I hand you over."

"Tell me about them."

Dollinger shared his story of the tidy little gook and his towering henchmen. The details were scant.

"I know who they might be," Levon said when Dollinger was done.

"Care to enlighten me, Mr. Holman?" Dollinger blinked.

"I don't know specifics. It's a foreign outfit with reach. I crossed their path a few years ago. And you're right, Dollinger. They're not the type to leave loose ends."

"Then I will be vanishing once again as of this morning for places unknown."

"You can finance a run?"

"They left me a card for essentials. I plan on heading farther west, Seattle or maybe Los Angeles, and using it to make the maximum cash withdraw and see how far that takes me."

"I have a better idea."

Dollinger leaned across the table with brows beetled and lips pursed.

"Make your withdraw here in Ketchum."

Dollinger sat back, his mouth agape.

"That'd bring them right down on you," he said, voice low and furtive.

"That's the way I want it," Levon said, eyes fixed past the man across the table. "Now you take off. And if I ever see you again, it won't matter how many people are around."

"I will receive that as gospel, Mr. Holman," Dollinger said and stood to walk away into the crowd lined up before the food trucks.

Merry and Hope rushed up to the table.

"Who was that?" Merry asked.

"Can we get another goat?" Hope asked simultaneously.

"Just a guy talking livestock prices," Levon said to Merry. And to Hope: "Have you got one picked out?"

The girls each took a hand to lead him back to the stock pens.

TAKE A LOOK AT: DROWNING ARE THE DEAD
BY BRENT TOWNS

BEST-SELLING AUTHOR BRENT TOWNS RETURNS WITH THIS PRIVATE DETECTIVE MYSTERY—FULL OF SMALL-TOWN SECRECY AND DEADLY INTRIGUE.

In the middle of Australia's Outback lies the small town of Friar's Lake. It's quaint, quiet, and—more importantly—devoid of crime.

So, when a body turns up with the hallmark signs of a manic serial killer from the past, Private Investigator Trent Jacobs is hired by a town local to find out if Ten Cent—the infamous killer—is back.

But as this once-quiet town begins to unravel, tragedy strikes again, and Trent goes missing.

Thankfully, newcomer Mark Hayes is eager to help out. Until—with every shocking secret that's uncovered, he begins to question whether he can find the killer before time runs out.

After all…beneath small-town Friar Lake's dusty exterior, there are hidden truths of which even the locals are unaware.

AVAILABLE NOW

ABOUT THE AUTHOR

Born and raised in Philadelphia, Chuck Dixon worked a variety of jobs from driving an ice cream truck to working graveyard at a 7-11 before trying his hand as a writer. After a brief sojourn in children's books he turned to his childhood love of comic books. In his thirty years as a writer for Marvel, DC Comics and other publishers, Chuck built a reputation as a prolific and versatile freelancer working on a wide variety titles and genres from Conan the Barbarian to SpongeBob SquarePants. His graphic novel adaptation of J.R.R. Tolkien's The Hobbit continues to be an international bestseller translated into fifty languages. He is the co-creator (with Graham Nolan) of the Batman villain Bane, the first enduring member added to the Dark Knight's rogue's gallery in forty years. He was also one of the seminal writers responsible for the continuing popularity of Marvel Comics' The Punisher.

After making his name in comics, Chuck moved to prose in 2011 and has since written over twenty novels, mostly in the action-thriller genre with a few side-trips to horror, hardboiled noir and western. The transition from the comics form to prose has been a life-altering event for him. As Chuck says, "writing a comic is like getting on a roller coaster while writing a novel is more like a long car trip with a bunch of people you'll learn to hate." His Levon Cade novels are currently in production as a television series from Sylvester Stallone's Balboa Productions. He currently lives in central Florida and, no, he does not miss the snow.